EVERY STEP YOU TAKE

A PSYCHOLOGICAL THRILLER

AVERY LANE

PROLOGUE

I keep thinking about the sound of her crying. Which is strange, because at the time, it didn't mean much to me. I was crying too. I wanted out just as bad as she did.

What I didn't realize was that I took those tears with me. I carried them in my heart. And without even realizing, I let those tears erode the muscle until I could no longer ignore the irreparable damage it had done to the way it beats.

I only let her go because I couldn't listen to her cry for another second. I couldn't bear it. Don't you know what it means to love someone this way?

1

R iley's breath caught as she felt the razor-thin metal swipe across the pad of her index finger.

So close. So effin' close.

Just a few millimeters more and she could secure some sort of grip on it.

But she could tell she was already in too precarious a position to go any further. A position that would certainly horrify all that cared for her safety.

She lowered herself carefully from her tip-toes, feeling the still plastic-wrapped phone book shift just slightly beneath her feet.

Oops, she thought, clenching her teeth. She held her breath, hoping her stillness would secure a stable position.

Riley looked down at her jury-rigged step-stool.

Atop the scooped out seat of her wooden dining chair, she had stacked three phonebooks she found in her building's lobby to give her the extra lift she needed to reach the top shelf of her kitchen cupboard. The shelf where her allergy medicine sat in their tinfoil sleeves, just out of reach.

But three phonebooks weren't enough. Not for the mere five feet she stood on a good day. So now she would be left to quietly rage, sleepless in her itchy-throated, watery-eyed frustration.

She hopped back down to the stability of her hardwood floors, standing arms akimbo as she looked up at the open cupboard.

Evan had purposely hidden her allergy medication all the way up there.

At the peak of their troubles, Riley found it difficult to fall asleep. And nothing "natural" helped. Not blackout curtains, not blindfolds, not warm milk or hot baths. Not even that extra glass of cabernet she had come to rely on.

But antihistamines *always* managed to knock her out.

Evan called it "drug abuse" because she wasn't taking the medication for its intended use. So he took her stash and put it in a place that she couldn't even reach with the help of a chair.

And while he wasn't entirely wrong, his true reason for hiding Riley's medication was not because he was concerned about her misuse. Evan just liked his role of dictator in their household of two. He liked the fact that he had near total power over another individual when he had zero control of his own mediocre life and for over a decade, he hid his controlling behavior under the guise of care.

Because for nearly the entire tenure of their relationship, Riley had no idea this was happening at all.

It all hit her one day – like a ton of bricks. In fact, it was only in that moment that Riley even understood the full meaning of that saying. The facts were there all along, collecting secretly in some safety net that hung above her head. Finally, one day, another random brick was tossed in – no different from any of the previous bricks. But it was the one that snapped that net. The one that gave her the courage to pack Evan's bags and set them outside their apartment door.

In the two months since he left, Riley had no trouble sleeping. But now that it was 2am and officially spring, Riley wished she had remembered earlier that he had sequestered her stash. The stash she now needed for its intended purposes.

Maybe some hot water. If she wasn't getting meds tonight, then she could perhaps scorch the irritation out of her throat.

She listened to the gas ticking and watched as a roar of flames flicked up around the kettle.

The sound reminded her of Evan – of those false recollections still erroneously filed under "good memories."

In their small, thin-walled one-bedroom, it was that sound that served as her morning alarm. He was always the one who made her coffee, and he always got it exactly how she liked it – light with two sugars. He sent her off to work with a packed breakfast every morning, usually a small mason jar of overnight oats topped with fresh blueberries or perfectly soft-boiled eggs. He had dinner ready when she got home, dinners that ranged from perfectly finished *sous vide* ribeyes to *cacio e pepe* so good, it rivaled her favorite Italian restaurants. He killed bugs, opened jars, fixed faucets, made sure the bills were paid. He could reach the top shelf of their absurdly high up kitchen cupboards.

From the outside, he was the perfect husband. He did *everything* for her.

And that was the point.

Evan made Riley so dependent on him that even now, out of the haze of what she finally understood to be an unhealthy, dysfunctional marriage, her coffee still never tasted quite right and any meal she tried to cobble together served as a reminder of how little she knew how to do.

She had lived three whole decades with no claim over her own life, no idea of who she was outside of the people she shared roofs with. In fact, Riley was pretty sure her chosen profession of event coordinator had everything to do with the fact that her subconscious understood her need for authority somewhere, *anywhere* in her day-to-day.

A low whine escaped from the kettle and Riley turned off the heat before it could reach its high-pitch wail.

She settled down on the couch with her cup of hot water, willing herself not to rub her eyes anymore than she already had.

Riley leaned back, forcing her raw eyelids to shut over the sticky grit of her allergy-ravaged eyeballs.

God, did she feel disgusting. And exhausted. All she wanted to do was sleep. But her nose was stuffy and every time she breathed in through her mouth, the fresh air just further irritated her throat.

She hoped the makeup she owned was heavy-duty enough to cover up the inevitable rings around her eyes.

Riley had been looking forward to the coming morning for months. After running her business from home for the last seven years, she was finally going to meet her first clients at a real, *actual* office. She had secured the location shortly after Evan left and though it was far from the glamorous location that Riley had always imagined, her assistant Marco had been slaving away the past week to make the space as presentable and professional as possible.

It felt like a momentous occasion. Having an actual office made Riley feel, well, official. Like her small business had suddenly been validated because it had its own address. But most importantly, it marked a new era for Riley – one where she could be a new person, perhaps someone closer to who she had always wanted to be. One where she could reimagine a future closer to the one that had previously only existed in her dreams.

Shhhkkkk.

Riley's eyes snapped open.

The strange sound had sliced through the silence of her apartment. She blinked, realizing only then that she had been dozing off.

Riley sat up, setting down her cup on the side table as she looked around.

It wasn't an entirely unfamiliar noise. In fact, Riley thought it sounded like a menu slipping under the front door. Every time someone in the building ordered delivery, the delivery guys would diligently clog everyone's doors with menus. Though she was just a bit cranky at having been woken up, Riley wasn't about to judge the person who ordered delivery at 2am in the middle of the week. It wasn't like she hadn't done it at least a handful of times since Evan left. It was just one of those perks of living in New York that everyone exploited.

She hopped up on her feet and made her way over.

Sure enough, something peeked out from under her front door. Riley's eyes were bleary from allergies and sleepiness, but it indeed looked like the corner of a menu. She picked it up.

The thick, plasticky surface struck her first. Then, the unusual weight and shape.

Riley ran her thumb over the white-framed black square in her hands.

She was looking at the back of a Polaroid picture.

Weird.

She turned it over.

At first, the photo didn't really strike her as anything at all. It looked like a picture that had been taken by accident, the way you would if you had dropped your phone with your camera on.

But this was a Polaroid.

Which meant that it took a little more effort to pop out a photo.

Suddenly, it struck her what she was looking at.

She squinted at the photo to make sure she was seeing right.

The lower third of the picture was the speckled tan floors of her apartment building's hallways. The upper two thirds were occupied by one of the green doors marking individual apartment units. The gold number nailed to the front was the number 7.

Her apartment number.

Her door.

A quick chill ran up her spine.

What in the hell?

Before she could think, Riley had already swung open her front door and plodded out in her slippers. Her body always reacted before her mind could. Had she stopped even for a second, she would have realized that running out at 2am into potential danger clad only in pajamas was probably a bad idea. Just like climbing up on your tiptoes atop poorly balanced phone books was a bad idea.

A draft crept up her flannel shorts.

There was no one there.

She rushed to the stairwell, leaning over the banister to look down towards the building's lobby. Riley stayed perfectly still, listening for footsteps.

Nothing.

All she could hear was the blood rushing in her ears. The pulsing hum of her heart against her ribcage. The faint whistle of a night breeze creeping through the cracks of their pre-war building.

She stepped back into her apartment, shutting the door behind her.

Every hair on her body was standing on end.

Her body knew to be scared, but as per usual, her brain hadn't caught up.

Her brain was just angry.

Evan.

Classic Evan.

She had blocked his number after he broke her "no contact without lawyers" rule by sending a steady stream of hundreds of repetitive texts, berating her for callously casting him out of her life when he had done nothing but "give her everything he had."

Please.

She set the Polaroid down on her kitchen counter, sucking in air through her teeth as she stopped herself from unblocking Evan's number just so she could scream at him.

It was then that she noticed something scribbled on the white frame of the photo, right where she had been gripping it.

A note.

She squinted at the smudged ballpoint handwriting.

We're never really alone.

2

Riley arrived at the office as put together as she could be considering the events of the previous night.

She was forced to let go of how she had envisioned this morning going as soon as she realized she'd be running on a collective hour or so of sleep.

Originally, she had considered making an event of this day.

Riley imagined waking up bright and early, taking a long luxurious shower, blowing out and flat-ironing her frizzy auburn hair, and putting on the sort of refined but understated makeup that all the young professional women in rom-coms always had on. She'd march into the office in her favorite emerald green blouse tucked into her black pencil skirt with a solid hour to admire the beginning of her new life before the clients even got in.

Instead, Riley struggled just to look halfway presentable.

With the help of some YouTube tutorials and color correction makeup she had bought years ago but never opened (and hoped wasn't somehow expired), she had managed to neutralize the purple rings around her eyes and the red blotches around her nose. It, however, did nothing for her weary expression, but she hoped the coffee she asked Marco to pick up for her would do the trick.

Her office was a finished corner on the second floor of a huge, mostly unoccupied four-story building that sat on the Gowanus Canal. Like many buildings in the neighborhood, it was an abandoned factory with aspirations of becoming high-end condos and retail space but was stuck in the purgatory of building permits and regulations.

Riley had snagged her steeply discounted office because her mother Judy was somehow good friends with the building owner's parents and trusted Riley to keep to her corner while they struggled with the logistics of finishing the building. So she happily became one of four questionably legal tenants in the very unfinished, barely occupiable building.

Her office was there along with a barebones café in the lobby, the curmudgeon of a CPA next to that, and the studio right below Riley's office – what she thought was perhaps a karate dojo judging from the war cries she often heard rattling through the vents.

At first, she had been reluctant to let her mother help her with anything. She was nervous that accepting aid from Judy invited her to poke at the boundaries that Riley had managed to set between them over the years.

And it was weird to even think that an elderly farm town hermit like Judy had any legitimate connections in the city at all. Even though Riley knew that Judy had lived in the city in her youth, the idea that *she* was the one who would ultimately find Riley her office space was still pretty mind-blowing.

Riley's heels echoed down the hall.

The second floor was not quite as finished as the lobby but looked a hell of a lot better than the two floors above it. There were still exposed steel beams outlining where the future offices would be along with some freshly plastered but unpainted walls. It was still far more professional than having clients meet her in cafes and having Marco take calls from his own cell phone while sitting on her couch at home. And it wasn't like she could afford anything else. She was lucky to have this space at all.

As she approached the door, she could hear Marco on the phone.

Riley smiled, feeling lucky to have such a diligent and hard-working assistant. Marco had been with her since he was a sophomore in college and at only twenty-three, carried himself with more professionalism and grace than Riley could ever imagine for herself. She would be envious of his put-togetherness if it didn't benefit her business so greatly.

Just when her hand wrapped around the doorknob, Riley made out a second voice on the other side. Her heart stopped.

Oh shit, the clients are early.

Riley took in a deep breath, trying to calm herself. She had really banked on having a little time to get to her coffee and settle in before having her meeting. She really needed it. But she settled on simply smoothing her hands over her hair, fanning it out as neatly as she could around her shoulders, and taking in a deep breath. Then she opened the door, mustering up her best smile.

Immediately, her smile fell.

"I'm so sorry," Marco sputtered upon seeing her. "I asked him to leave."

His wiry frame looked tense in his fitted white button-down. His normally tidy black undercut was becoming undone. He clutched a binder to his chest, as if it were a shield.

Across from him stood a man facing away from her. He didn't have to turn for her to know who it was.

Evan had never really ever been an intimidating looking man. He was tallish, skinny, wore his dirty blond hair messy like a college kid. But Evan's innocuous appearance was always part of his danger. It was what allowed people like him to get away with the terrible things they did.

Today though...

Today, Evan *looked* like a physical threat. The oversized black sweatshirt he wore bulked up his lanky body, making his frame hang and hover in a menacing manner. His body was tense, stiff, on edge. As he turned, he remained backlit by the windows behind him, his silhouette fusing with the dark, looming shadow he casted over Riley.

She found herself face-to-face with what felt like a humanoid black hole.

She swallowed hard, trying to regain the bearings she never had.

"You blocked my number," he replied. His voice was hoarse. He looked like he had aged ten years in the two months they hadn't seen each other.

She stared up at him, her gaze unwavering. Riley summoned all the anger she harbored towards him, pulling from the depths of her soul. She thought about the ominous note that Evan had slipped her last night – the one that had ruined any chance for sleep. She thought about how he was continuing to ruin her day now.

Riley could feel her feet spreading and her elbows point out as she put her hands on her hips to make herself look bigger. She wasn't going to stand for this another second.

"Get out of my office, Evan," she said. Her voice was still high-pitched and girly, but there was a gravitas in it that Riley hadn't heard before. *I can do this,* she thought. *I drove him out once before and I can do it again.*

"You didn't even give us a chance," Evan said, ignoring her. His eyes were bloodshot. Riley could smell alcohol on his breath. "We need to really sit down and talk about this. You're being unreasonable, you know. We need to just talk this out."

"There's nothing to talk out," Riley scoffed.

"You didn't even tell me what the problem was! You didn't even tell me what I did wrong, what I did to deserve this. Don't you owe me that much?" Riley blinked at Evan's ridiculous question. It took everything in her not to roll her eyes.

"I don't owe you anything," Riley replied. "And you know what this is about. Just because you got away with it for as long as you did doesn't mean that an explanation is suddenly needed."

"Riley, without me, you would never even have this place," Evan seethed. "I supported you financially, emotionally, *physically* while you built this little business of yours. Do you think you could've done *any* of this without me?"

"That's for the lawyers to figure out," Riley said, her voice more callous now. Out of the corner of her eye, she caught a glimpse of Marco covering his mouth, just watching. "Now get out of here so I can get to work."

"You don't mean that." Evan's voice softened. It was the same voice he used every time they came close to arguing in the past. It was meant to manipulate Riley into feeling like *she* was the one in the wrong, like she was the one who had been hurting *him* all along. But that wasn't going to work anymore.

"Evan, please, I have a job to do," she said. "I'll see you again when the papers are ready."

"I'm not signing those papers until you give us one more chance. One *real* chance. You never even gave me a choice in this, Riley. You just made this decision that we were over, just like that! Without me. I am your husband, for God's sake. Your partner."

"So what, I made a decision without you just this once?" Riley arched an eyebrow. "Kind of like you've been doing our entire time together, right?"

Evan sighed, lowering his gaze. His shoulders slumped.

He ducked his head, allowing a halo of light to be cast atop his blond mop of hair. Everything he did was calculated. Riley couldn't believe it took her almost a decade to truly see through him.

"You're right," Evan said. "I did do that. I know. I can see where I was wrong now. There were a lot of things I should've done differently and all I'm asking is that you give me a chance to change things and make things right. Please. I know I hurt you but I can make up for all of it and more. I really can. Let me show you. What do you say?"

He took her hands into his, squeezing them just tight enough so that his wedding ring dug into her knuckles.

It was then that he noticed she wasn't wearing hers.

She watched the realization flicker across his face.

"That should answer your question," Riley replied. Her voice was steady now, icy and resolved. "Now get the hell out of my office before I call the cops."

She looked past Evan to see Marco pick up the landline, completely ready to dial 911.

The slight motion infuriated Evan, as if he had only then remembered that there was someone else in the room.

He leaped towards Marco's desk, grabbing Marco's hand and slamming down the receiver, knocking over the steaming hot cup of coffee that sat beside it.

The liquid splashed up around them before settling in a dark puddle on the hardwood floors.

"Evan, leave!" Riley screamed. She had lost any sense of control of her voice. She sounded desperate now, like a scared child. She mashed 911 into her phone, her hands shaking, before turning it to show Evan how serious she was. "Leave, or I will make sure there's a police record of you trespassing, assaulting my assistant, and threatening me. Do you understand?"

A heavy silence permeated the room, and for a second, it felt as if the world had frozen around her.

Then Riley watched as a dozen different expressions flashed across Evan's face before it finally settled on a deep contempt.

"How do you plan on affording your life without my half of the bills?" Evan asked, seething. "How do you plan on continuing to pay for your little business and your little assistant while keeping a roof over your head? You *need* me. Do *you* understand?"

"I don't need you, Evan." Riley stepped aside, pointing at the door. "And I never will again. Now. Leave."

Evan stood stoic for a beat before a nasty grin spread across his face.

And then, a deafening crack.

Splinters of wood shot into the air.

Riley flinched, shrinking down into the ground as she instinctively covered her head.

Of all the things Evan did to her, he had never been violent before. Through her shaking, she tried to understand what had just happened. She felt numb. There was no pain anywhere in her body.

Only then did she realize that Evan had put all his force into kicking up the repurposed antique chair that sat in their waiting area – a favorite piece of hers that she had brought in from the apartment. Evan knew this. He had fought Riley hard when she first brought it into their home – one of the few purchases she had dared to make without consulting him first.

Riley straightened up, staring at its remnants, her feet unmoving.

It was only a chair that he had chosen to destroy, but one swift kick had completely disassembled it. He clearly wanted Riley to know what he was capable of.

This was a not so thinly veiled threat.

Evan skulked over to her, bending over so that his lips were millimeters from her ear.

"You can stop your strong, independent woman act, Riley," he hissed. "We both know this isn't real."

He grabbed the doorknob, swinging the door open so forcefully that it slammed against the wall with an explosive bang. Riley could just about hear the metal doorknob denting.

Then he charged out.

She forced her head to turn in his direction, to watch him leave, as if to make sure it was actually happening. The adrenaline was still coursing through Riley's veins.

She watched as he blew down the hallway, passing the faces of a man and woman, eyes wide as they stared at the spectacle, right before the door creaked shut again.

The clients.

Shit.

They had heard everything.

3

Riley played with the pendant dangling from the silver chain she wore around her wrist. Keeping her hands busy somehow helped her focus as she listened to her new clients talk about all the things they wanted in their dream wedding. Though the couple had mercilessly pretended they hadn't seen anything, Riley was more than aware of the fact that they had at least *heard* everything.

She sure hoped she had a second chance at a first impression.

Not that it would be *that* much better looking as shaken and unkempt as she did right now. And *definitely* not compared to the ridiculously attractive couple that now sat across from her.

Sierra and Brighton were both thirty-five and both getting married for the very first time. Though it was typical of career-focused New York for people to marry late, Riley imagined it had to have been an active struggle for these two considering the absolute marriage material they appeared to be.

Sierra was 5'10" and willowy, effortlessly gorgeous in her floral print maxi dress and cropped, tan leather jacket. Her long, wavy black hair perfectly framed sharp, emerald green eyes and sun-kissed cheekbones. If she hadn't modeled at some point in her life, she definitely could have. Hell, she could probably still get signed if she just walked into an agency right that second.

Brighton was her perfect counterpart. He was just over six feet tall with sandy-colored hair worn longish and casually swept back. A close-cut beard framed a chiseled jawline and a shy, thoughtful smile. He let Sierra do most of the talking as his crystal blue eyes watched over her with the sort of longing that belied their decade-long relationship.

It was almost a joke how perfect they were. They looked like they should be wearing all white and lounging on a private beach in the Maldives, feeding each other figs or something – not sitting in Riley's dinky little office and staring at her like she had any sort of answers for them.

Riley could feel the slightest hint of envy percolating in her empty stomach.

No amount of contouring would give Riley Sierra's bone structure and there was no chance in hell she'd miraculously grow ten inches in her thirties. And Riley was *at least* a decade if not a lifetime out from developing the sort of elegant composure Sierra had – the kind that just screamed the self-assuredness of true adulthood. Riley was woefully behind the average woman in that department, and even more so behind someone like Sierra.

She eyed Sierra's ring finger. The engagement ring was pretty unconventional, though that seemed to be the trend these days. It was a thick blonde wood band, polished to glint like gold. Where the diamond would normally be was an inset holding a dark, smoky, princess-cut stone that caught the light as well as any of its more established counterparts.

Riley put her hands under the desk. Even before seeing Sierra's sophisticated choice in jewelry, she had felt self-conscious of her chunky silver bracelet. She often found that it looked childish and perhaps even a bit tacky. But despite that, Riley had a really hard time ever taking that bracelet off. Her father had made it for her with his own two hands. Her name was engraved on the pendant. It was her only real connection to him.

"So...we want to get married before the end of June."

Riley blinked, shaken from her own thoughts.

Marco was taking notes, *thank God*, considering how distracted Riley had been throughout everything Sierra was saying. She realized then that she had absorbed literally nothing. At least not until this last sentence.

It was April 3rd. That meant not even three months to plan a wedding in the middle of wedding season.

Suddenly, it was clear to Riley why someone like Sierra went for an event planner of her tier. Everyone above her would have already been booked. And if they weren't, they would've laughed Sierra out of their offices.

"So...?" Sierra raised her perfectly shaped eyebrows. "Do you think that's possible?"

"It's...possible," Riley said, though she wasn't really sure. She mostly specialized in one-off corporate events because weddings came with a whole slew of emotional investment and socialization that Evan never really allowed. So with only a handful of weddings under her belt, none of which only gave her three months to plan, Riley couldn't be confident that this was going to go well under her care. "But if we're going to proceed, I'll need to temper your expectations."

"Of course," Sierra nodded. "I totally understand."

"You're probably not going to get exactly what you were hoping for. There will be compromises and complications. There always are, but there will be even more because it's a wedding on short notice with a significant guest list. And unfortunately, it may cost you a good amount more as well."

"Got it," Sierra said, holding her hands up in front of her. "Of course."

"And we would have to get started as soon as possible."

"Definitely, definitely." Sierra nodded, her eyes wide and eager. Riley couldn't help but laugh. The fact that a woman like Sierra was treating Riley like an authority figure of any kind was kind of hilarious to her. Whatever impression she had made on them was apparently good enough to earn their trust. For the first time in awhile, it seemed like luck was on her side.

"Okay, so I think I can help you," Riley replied.

"Oh my goodness, yes!" Sierra jumped to her feet, clapping her hands together before reaching behind her for Brighton. He took her hand, getting up to stand by her side.

The picture-perfect couple embraced. And now that they were officially clients, Riley found their picture-perfectness a little less upsetting.

"Thank you," Brighton said, breaking his silence. Riley smiled at him, wondering what it was like to have a husband so happy to let his wife call all the shots.

She switched her gaze back to Sierra.

"So...um, may I ask what the rush is?" Riley watched as Sierra and Brighton exchanged another meaningful glance.

"Well," Sierra started, as if they had silently made the decision that she would continue to speak for them. "We want our dream wedding, for sure. But only because we want the photos to show our future children. And we definitely don't want to wait another second to start our family. So we thought we'd better get this show on the road."

"That's..." Riley began. A genuine smile swept across her face. "That's lovely." She could feel a deep warmth radiating from her heart. It was the first positive sensation her poor little heart had felt in over twenty-four hours.

4

It was 11am but Riley thought Marco deserved the rest of the day off.

Hell, Riley was thinking she might just do the same.

But first, coffee.

Thanks to Evan's surprise visit, the coffee Marco had ready for her was currently soaking into her office floors. And despite the fact that Riley planned on eschewing her workday, she still needed the caffeine for the walk home.

The café downstairs hadn't bothered to name itself, probably because they had been given the same uncertain pseudo-lease that Riley was given. There was no real décor and the silver, circular dining tables and red, vinyl upholstered stools that spotted their cement floors looked older than the space itself – definitely diner hand-me-downs they had found off Craigslist.

And as was the case for places like this, it was cash only.

Riley rifled through her purse, wondering if she actually had the cash she needed to pay for her almond milk latte and bacon and egg croissant. Paper money seemed like such a relic to her now. And looking through her purse was kind of a false gesture – she knew there was no way in hell she had ten whole bucks in there.

Riley put a pathetic handful of change on the counter, leftovers from the last time she was forced to use cash. It dawned on her that she might not be getting her coffee and breakfast after all, which honestly, seemed like an appropriate return to Riley's sort of luck.

"May I?"

The question rumbled out of an imposing figure behind her. She turned, but carefully, realizing just how close she was to the eclipse of a man that had approached the counter.

Riley tipped her head back, farther and farther, looking up for what felt like forever before she could even detect a face. She heard the sound of something slip across the counter and she whipped her head back down and around to see the ten-dollar bill pinned underneath a strong hand.

The barista took the cash without question and the man stepped back just enough so that Riley could get a comfortable look at him.

The dark-haired mountain smiled at her, moving to cross his arms as he surveyed her with amusement. For a suspenseful second, Riley wondered if a man with biceps and pecs his size could even cross his arms comfortably. But he managed, and he looked plenty comfortable.

"Thank you," she muttered, still taking in the view.

Evan was the only man she had ever been with, and for the entirety of their relationship, she never wondered about other guys. Perhaps it was because Evan had effectively closed her off from meeting new people outside of work and even then, closely monitored her client relationships. And after an incident where Evan accused her of wanting to cheat on him, simply because Riley had looked at some movie poster with Ryan Gosling for a second longer than she should have, she had managed to train herself not to regard any man in such a way ever again.

But now...now she was in the clear to look again.

"I'm Gabriel," the man said, extending his hand for a shake. Riley's own hand hardly took up the surface of his palm.

Gabriel's hands were surprisingly rough and calloused for someone as well groomed as he looked. His nails appeared manicured, his skin was smooth and evenly tanned, and Riley could smell the foresty scent of his body wash. His charcoal tri-blend t-shirt and fitted dark-wash jeans looked freshly laundered.

"Riley," she replied, clearing her throat so she could regain a more stately sounding voice. "I'm Riley."

"Riley," Gabriel repeated. His eyebrows lifted in tandem with a teasing lilt in his voice. A playful smile showed off a set of perfect teeth. His giant physique was suddenly less intimidating.

"I, um, I can pay you back for the food," Riley stuttered. "I just don't normally carry cash, you know? I can Venmo you. Or, well, if you prefer cash I can have cash next time. Do you come here a lot?"

"I do," Gabriel shrugged. "But you don't have to pay me back."

"Oh no, I can't..." Riley said. "I can't accept that. And I'm perfectly capable of paying for my own food. Just a bit unprepared today."

"Consider this a gift," Gabriel smiled.

"I can't." Riley shook her head.

"Why?" Gabriel looked a bit insulted now, or maybe confused.

"I just, you know, I don't like..." Riley began to explain, feeling a bit silly now. "I don't want anyone's *help* anymore."

"Anymore?"

"I mean, at all," Riley shook her head. "Not 'anymore.' I meant 'at all.' I don't want – I mean, I don't *need* anyone's help. Not that I don't appreciate...your help."

"Alright," Gabriel laughed. "Then pay me back. Whatever. It'll be a nice excuse to see you again."

Riley furrowed her brows.

Oh, she thought. *Was this...?*

Flirting.

She had never really done it as an adult.

Suddenly, she was blushing furiously.

And she could *tell* it was a furious blush by Gabriel's reaction. His lips curled up in amusement.

"You can pay me back tonight," Gabriel said. "Over dinner or something."

"Oh."

This was too much. Her morning had gone from a total disaster to a peculiar stroke of good luck, then back to a tiny bit more of bad luck, and now she was being asked out on a date? Riley wasn't ready to date. In fact, she couldn't be farther from it. She barely knew who she was outside of being Evan's wife and she hadn't yet had a chance to, *I don't know,* self-develop.

But you didn't say no to a man who looked like Gabriel, right? She had never really dated, but she knew that these sort of men could not be easy to come by. Especially for someone as dowdy and average as she knew she was.

Wait. Was that something to be suspicious of? A man clearly out of her league who just upped and paid for her breakfast then proceeded to ask her to dinner?

Maybe she was underestimating her value in the dating market. Or maybe Gabriel had no idea what he looked like. But judging from the way the baristas and café patrons were staring at him, Riley figured that was unlikely.

"Okay, sure," Riley blurted out.

Oh my God, her brain screamed. *I wasn't done analyzing this!* She could feel her mind continuing to protest, furious at the words that had managed to escape her mouth. But it was too late. Gabriel was already putting his number in her phone.

You can still say no, you can put a stop to this!

Riley smiled, letting out a small laugh at the war between her brain and her body. When Gabriel returned the smile, his gorgeous eyes crinkling in delight, Riley already knew her body would sure as hell be going on this date even if her mind didn't want to.

5

The air was still and crisp, just warm enough that an evening amble through Park Slope seemed like the perfect idea.

Keeping things casual also helped with Riley's nerves.

Riley wished she had the luxury of consulting someone over her chosen outfit, but having friends wasn't exactly something Riley excelled in. Evan was meant to serve as an all-in-one. He was at once a husband and a best friend by default. He had his own friends that sometimes served as Riley's social circle, but that was really it. If it weren't for Marco, Riley knew that these past two months would have been nothing but pure isolation and loneliness.

Marco would probably be happy to pick an outfit out for Riley. Though he was mostly reserved and quiet, he had always dressed impeccably and had that classic sort of good taste that Riley always admired. But she wasn't about to subject him to anymore of her personal life. At least not today.

So Riley decided to mimic Sierra's outfit as best she could with what she had available. She owned a floral dress, but like many of the things she wore, it looked a bit childish – like the sort of thing Judy used to put her in on picture day. The print was pink and pastel, unlike the bold violets and junipers on Sierra's dress. But it was all she really had that was appropriate for a springtime date.

Because she didn't own a lick of leather, she topped the dress with a white lace cardigan and prayed that the right makeup and hair would save her from looking like she was heading to church.

There was so much time and thought put into her outfit, hair, and makeup that she just about guffawed when Gabriel arrived wearing the same exact outfit he had on when they met earlier that day.

All eyes were on them as they strolled down Fifth Avenue. And there were plenty of people out on this beautiful spring evening. Riley couldn't help but wonder what it was that drew those glances when she was far more used to being overlooked. At her diminutive size, she had even gotten used to getting elbowed in the face by taller people who didn't even realize she was behind them.

So it was more than unusual to know that she suddenly had everyone's attention. She considered, just briefly, that this was the result of her disastrous choice in dressing herself. Or maybe she had inadvertently broken some sort of date rule with her hair up in a ponytail. But realistically, she knew it wasn't anything about her that was drawing all the stares.

They're staring because Gabriel's a giant. And a gorgeous giant, at that. One that didn't seem to mind that the contents of his taco were tumbling down the front of his shirt.

Riley smiled. That was definitely it. People were staring because of the wildly handsome and surprisingly adorable man standing beside her. And rather than be uncomfortable with that, she should be happy that she was lucky enough to land him. And just two months into being single.

Over the course of a dozen blocks, Riley learned that Gabriel had graduated college a year early and spent the past decade traveling the world as a camera operator for an eccentric trust fund baby with aspirations of making the "next groundbreaking documentary." Gabriel was compensated well and enjoyed what felt like paid vacations, but thousands of hours of footage later, they never actually completed a single project.

And as fun as all that was, he found himself yearning for some-thing to show for his efforts. So he returned to New York to start his own business.

Gabriel was the man responsible for the war cries that Riley heard rumbling through the vents. He ran a parkour studio, one that had gotten increasingly popular due to its vast space and the creatively challenging obstacles that Gabriel had designed.

"So what you're hearing is grown men doing back flips off fifteen-foot walls," Gabriel said, disposing of his taco wrapper as he patted the food off the front of his shirt.

"And they like...land on their feet?" Riley frowned. She couldn't imagine how that would work.

"No," Gabriel laughed. "At least not most of them. I have like a pit of foam for them to land in."

"What made you decide to open a parkour studio of all things? Why not videography since that's what you've been doing?"

"My favorite part of what I did wasn't the camera stuff. It was all the climbing around to get good shots," he replied. "So when I got home, I thought – what if all I did was *just* the climbing? So, bam. Parkour studio."

"Interesting train of thought," Riley smiled. She thought about Evan and his obsession with American Ninja Warrior. He was nowhere close to athletic, but it would've been a dream of his to own a parkour studio. Or any business at all. He never considered what Riley had to be a legitimate business and insisted on correcting her every time she would refer to her work as such. He took any chance he had to tell her that she was "just a freelancer" and that she didn't have the chops to be more than that.

It was a big part of what drove her to find herself an office. Riley supposed she should thank Evan for that.

"So how about you? What's life like as an event planner?"

"It's lot of phone calls," Riley started. "And organizing and bossing people around. There's a bunch of paperwork. It's fast-paced. There are deadlines. Tons of pressure."

"Your dream job, I'm assuming."

"Yes, actually," Riley smiled. "I know that was a joke, but it feels like you have me figured out." Gabriel looked pleased with himself, the way a kid might look after finishing a particularly difficult puzzle.

"I think I have a good sense of who you are."

"Is it good or bad, what you sense?"

"Obviously good or we wouldn't be on a date right now."

"You know, when you said we'd be going to dinner, I actually thought we'd be sitting down at a restaurant somewhere."

"Oh, what? You didn't like the taco truck?" Gabriel put a hand over his chest, like he was wounded by this.

"No, it's good!" Riley laughed. "This is good. It's, I don't know, less pressure?"

"I thought you just said you were into being under pressure."

"Yes, but only at work," Riley answered. "I'm a very different person at work versus not at work."

Gabriel stopped walking, turning towards Riley to look at her with a thoughtfulness she couldn't understand. There was a soft expression on his face.

Riley was intrigued. And flattered. There was something about his gaze that made her feel fascinating. Like nothing she had ever felt before.

A dreamy, bell-like melody suddenly surrounded her and it was only then that she realized they were stopped in front of an ice cream truck. She wanted to be embarrassed, but instead, she laughed at herself, peering up through her lashes as she watched Gabriel pull out a wad of cash.

"We want ice cream, right?" he asked. "I don't want to speak for you, but I'm just getting these ice cream vibes." He flipped open the wad, flipping quickly through a bunch of singles.

"Do you moonlight as a stripper?" Riley teased. "I imagine you'd do well."

"I appreciate the compliment," Gabriel replied, cracking a smile. "But I'm just the type that carries cash around."

"I feel like our generation just, you know, does everything electronically so it's kind of weird that you do."

"I think you maybe mistaken about us being from the same generation," Gabriel said. Riley hadn't considered that. Gabriel didn't look old at all. She had just assumed they were the same age.

"So...how old are you?"

"Thirty-six," he replied. "Is that okay?"

"Oh, sure," Riley said. That was barely different from her thirty-one years, but she recognized that the five years between them might've meant a significant distinction in their technological behavior. "Don't you want to know how old I am?"

"I assume of age because you own your own business."

"There are literal children running companies in Silicon Valley, I think it's best you ask."

"Isn't it rude to ask women how old they are?"

"Why are you so old-school? You're only four years older than I am!"

"Alright, so you're thirty-one," Gabriel said. "Clearly, it was very important for you that I know that. Now what ice cream do you want?"

"Strawberry shortcake, please."

"A sophisticated choice."

"You're mocking me."

"No, I'm really not," Gabriel replied. "Because I'm ordering one of those Spongebob bars with the gumball eyes."

Riley watched as Gabriel put in their order, totally straight-faced. He wasn't kidding about the Spongebob bar. As he counted out the cash to pay, Riley pressed a fresh ten-dollar bill into his hand.

"For this morning," Riley said.

"Oh, damn," Gabriel replied. "You weren't kidding about paying me back."

"Why would I be kidding?"

"I don't know, I thought it was banter."

"Maybe it was a little bit banter," Riley replied. "But it was mostly a new policy of mine. Accepting help has only ever bit me in the ass. But you did come to my aid in my time of need and I thank you for that. And now we're even."

"Fine," Gabriel laughed. He pocketed the money before taking their popsicles and resuming their walk. He held the strawberry shortcake out towards Riley. "Just FYI, I'll do better on our next date. I'm seeing now how bad tacos and popsicles look."

"Next date?" Riley arched an eyebrow.

"Oh please, you know you like me." He took a bite out of his popsicle.

"Of course," Riley smiled, taking her own popsicle from him. "How could I not?" She just didn't realize he liked her back just as much.

"So," Gabriel said. "Tell me how a girl from upstate turns into the Type A businesswoman you are today."

Riley furrowed her brows.

Something about the sentence struck her as odd.

It took her a good long second before she realized what it was.

"How'd you know I'm from upstate?" she asked. Riley had told him a bunch of things over the course of the night, but she was pretty sure she hadn't mentioned that. She kind of didn't like mentioning where she was from. But she wracked her brain, wondering if she was wrong.

Gabriel didn't answer.

She looked up at him, waiting.

He continued walking in silence, his jaw clenched shut.

Every beat that went by made Riley feel more on edge.

"Sorry," he said, finally. He held his popsicle out to show Riley. Spongebob was missing an eye. "I just got the gumball unexpectedly and it got stuck in my teeth."

"Oh." Riley let out a hesitant laugh. That explained the pause, but not how he knew she was from upstate.

"Your phone number," Gabriel replied. He blew a perfectly round bubble before popping the gum and sucking it back into his mouth. "845. That's an upstate area code."

"Oh!" Riley exclaimed. She wrapped her free hand over her forehead. "I'm an idiot, duh."

"What, you thought I was some creep?"

"For a second, yeah."

"Hmm," he responded, his lips pressed into a straight line.

"Sorry. For thinking you were a creep." Riley frowned.

"It's fine."

The atmosphere thickened with an unbearable awkwardness.

Riley gritted her teeth. *Well, there goes the night.*

"I'm sorry," Riley said again. "We were having such a good time and I just ruined it." She could feel her stomach turn. She was suddenly very aware of the taco sitting inside it.

"No, of course not," Gabriel shook his head, stopping to put a hand on Riley's shoulder. "I'm *still* having a great time, I swear."

"You know, ugh. I shouldn't say this, but maybe it's a bit early for me to be dating again. Maybe that's why I'm acting like this."

"What do you mean?"

"I didn't want to mention this, but you actually caught me at kind of a weird time in my life," Riley continued. She didn't want to be saying these words, but they wouldn't stop. "I'm actually technically... married. But separated. My husband left two months ago. I saw him for the first time this morning and it kind of threw me off my game. He's also acting even worse than usual, so I don't even know how to deal. And what I was used to already sucked."

Shit.

Boy, she could babble when she wanted to. She could feel her mind screaming at her tongue, begging it not to continue. *Oh my God, stop it, seriously.*

Riley had committed a massive first date faux pas by subjecting Gabriel to ex drama. She didn't need a rich history of dating to know that much. And now, so she wouldn't keep going, she was waist-deep in the gravid, awkward silence it had created.

Gabriel furrowed his brows, looking concerned.

Change the subject, Riley thought. *Maybe bore him with thorough details of your seasonal allergies. Dear God, I shouldn't be allowed out of the house.*

"Did he...hurt you?" Gabriel asked. "Like, physically?"

"Oh, no. It was nothing like that," Riley replied. She didn't want to mention the chair. Not after all she had already said. She had just met the man and she was already forcing him to worry for her.

"You wouldn't lie about that, would you?"

"Definitely not," she said. "He'd never lay a hand on me. Can we talk about something else? I really hate that I mentioned any of this at all."

"If this happened just today, it's kinda fresh, isn't it? You're not really going to enjoy yourself until you get it off your chest," Gabriel said. "And I want you to enjoy yourself. For purely selfish reasons."

"Ha," Riley smiled, feeling a bit relieved. "Fine. But first, just to make me feel less awkward, you need to tell me why *you* ended your last relationship."

"Hmm." Gabriel's eyes crinkled thoughtfully. "The last girl I dated was back when we were working in Australia. She was a chef. She threw her favorite knife at me and then made me pay for it because it got damaged when I ducked and it hit the wall behind me."

"Um, wow." Riley blinked.

"Did you know knives can get really expensive?" he asked. Riley shook her head. "Anyway, I'm more than familiar with the crazies."

"Evan was a different kind of crazy, though," Riley explained. She took a deep breath. *Guess I'm doing this after all.* "He was controlling, but did it in a stealthy way so that I didn't realize until it was too late. My only friends were his friends. He made sure of that. He dictated what I ate by cooking every meal for me and got cranky if I ever wanted to deviate. While I was building my business, he was most of our income. But then my business got going and I quickly caught up to him. Even surpassed him a little. He didn't like that he couldn't control my work and it was then that I realized I let it all happen again."

"Let what happen again?"

"My mother was like this too," Riley sighed. Her brain had given up on telling her to shut up. She was clearly not shutting up. "It's a little different of course, because I was a kid for most of my time with her so I'd obviously *need* her help and guidance. But it went beyond that. She was an unbelievably oppressive presence in my life, beyond your typical helicopter parent. If she could've controlled the rate at which I breathed, I think she would have."

"I'm sure it was out of love."

"If she loved me, she would have realized she was suffocating me," Riley said.

"And your dad?"

"I never knew him. He died while my mom was pregnant, right before her fortieth birthday. They were 'older' parents and I was unplanned. So was his death. All the surprises and stress made her go into labor early. I was a little over two months premature. I was tiny when I was born and I guess I never really caught up. Genetically, I should be at *least* average height. But as you can see, I remain a bit vertically challenged."

"Being tall isn't so great," Gabriel said. "I have to duck to get out of the subway and sometimes I don't duck enough and I hit my head."

"Would you prefer that or being face-to-butt with people for ten stops?"

"Hmm. Tough call."

"Anyway," Riley smiled. "Now that you embarrassingly know my whole life story, it's your turn. What were your parents like? Where'd you grow up?"

"I grew up in New York. My parents were the complete opposite of controlling. They were hippies that let me and my brothers do whatever we wanted and never had any sort of meaningful advice for me."

"That kind of sounds amazing."

"Only people who didn't have those kind of parents would say that," Gabriel laughed. "I had zero direction in life and was constantly scared because of it. There was never any order or routine. And any question I had for my parents were met with some Bohemian non-answer. For the longest time, life was nothing but a scary uncertainty."

"Huh," Riley frowned. "Well. It seemed to work for you okay."

"Eventually, I learned from my brothers to embrace it. Which is how I ended up traveling the world with no goal or endgame for as long as I did."

"And you think you're done with that?"

"At least for now," Gabriel replied. "If I do it again, I want it to be with someone. You know, like a wife. And maybe children."

"Marriage and kids," Riley nodded. "We're just mentioning all those things we're not supposed to mention on a first date."

"I'd say this was a pretty successful first date *because* of all the over-sharing, not despite it. Wouldn't you?"

"I don't know," Riley teased. "I'm still feeling kind of nauseous from airing all that out."

"What, so you're not enjoying yourself?" Gabriel looked at her with feigned hurt. "Is it because I asked you out on a weeknight and took you to a taco truck? I thought self-employed people had no concept of weekends and liked eating on the go, so I thought it'd be okay."

"It was okay." Riley pressed her lips together, looking up at her mammoth of a date. She did think it went pretty well, but she felt like she'd be jinxing it to say it aloud. "A little more than okay, actually." The answer seemed to satisfy Gabriel. "But I think we should end the night here. I have to get to work early."

"Aw, alright. Where do you live?" he asked. "Can I walk you home?"

"No, I'm fine on my own."

"Even if I insist?"

"I'll get mad if you insist," Riley said. "I think you've learned enough about me today to know that."

"Fine," Gabriel sighed in an exaggerated manner. "If you insist that I don't insist, then I won't insist." Riley smiled. That was exactly the perfect amount of insistence.

6

P rospect Heights was a lovely, idyllic neighborhood with its wide, tree-lined streets and charming little shops and restaurants. It was mostly populated with young families that frequented the nearby park with their strollers and baby carriers.

But family-oriented neighborhoods often got quiet at night.

Riley normally liked that. It meant tranquil sleep conditions and a peaceful sense of being away from the city while never actually leaving.

But she rarely ever got home past 11pm and now that it was closing in on midnight, Riley was surprised with *just* how quiet it could be. Past Flatbush Avenue where the cars constantly zoomed in steady streams, the smaller side streets were awfully still. An occasional car would go by, but there wasn't a single pedestrian out besides Riley.

As she walked down Saint Marks, she noted that the street lamps were dimmer than she'd like and the sidewalk wasn't as smooth as it could be. She cursed the thick platforms of her sandals and how they kept her from getting a good feel for the ground beneath her. Riley listened to their heavy clomps, convinced she was going to trip at any second.

She should've called an Uber.

Riley stopped, whipping out her phone and wondering if Uber drivers were willing to do three-block rides.

But then she noticed the sound of her footsteps had continued without her.

Riley's head snapped up, looking around. She hadn't noticed anyone out on the block, but with all the garbage cans on the curb, she figured a straggler was just putting out their bin.

But she hadn't heard the bin being dragged out. And the footsteps continued for longer than it would take to get from a front door to the curb.

Riley squinted into the darkness, trying to make out any movement at all. But all she saw were the distant, fleeting lights of the traffic on Flatbush. She turned back towards the direction of home, picking up her pace just a bit. Her footsteps suddenly sounded louder, more distinct.

She turned onto a better-lit street, one that took her away from the direction of home. Riley wasn't sure why she made that decision. As always, her body moved faster than her mind, and it had decided on instinct that this was the right way to go.

Riley stood in front of a restaurant's windows, glancing back in the direction she came.

On the other side of the window, servers and busboys were winding down on their night, laughing as they cleaned. They looked relaxed, unaware of the panicked woman standing on the other side.

She was being paranoid.

Riley knew that.

But she couldn't help it. And could anyone really blame her?

Her soon-to-be ex-husband had threatened her that morning and she had received a cryptic photograph and note the night before. Granted, she had already concluded that the note was from Evan, but she hadn't recovered from the shock of it.

Just as Riley felt ready to start walking again, a dark figure suddenly appeared at the corner she had just left.

She was about a hundred feet away from that point now and she could barely make out the shadow's outline. The allergy medication she had finally bought and taken that morning was wearing off and her eyes were already tearing up, obscuring her night vision even further.

What she could see was that the figure was tall, a little hunched over. Kind of the way Evan looked at the office that morning.

A rush of anger came over her.

How dare he?

Had he followed her on her date? Had he been following her all day?

She ducked in the small alcove of the restaurant's front door. Safely out of sight, she flicked open her phone and scrolled through her contacts to Evan's number.

She unblocked him.

Then she called him, eyes fixed on the shadow at the intersection.

The phone rang just once before he picked up.

"Riley? Riley!" Evan called through the phone.

Riley could only hear Evan's voice coming from the speaker of her phone and not from the direction of the dark figure. She stayed silent, watching as the dark figure skulked around, as if looking for her.

But no light of a phone illuminated the shadow. No hand was lifted to its ear. No sound was coming from its direction.

It wasn't Evan.

So who was it?

7

"Thank you for saving my ass, I've been such a mess."

Riley heaved a heavy sigh, walking into her apartment as Marco followed.

When the shadow finally left, walking in the opposite direction of Riley's home, she made a mad rush towards her building only to find that she didn't have her keys.

She had somehow managed to lose them at some point in her unfortunate day.

Luckily, a neighbor who was taking his dog out had at least gotten her into the building or she would've had a full on panic attack. From the lobby, sitting on the stack of leftover phone books, she called Marco to bring the spare keys that she had taken from Evan and given to him for safekeeping.

Thank God she did.

"It's no problem," Marco said. "I'm glad I was nearby so I could get here quick. I feel so bad you're having like the worst day ever."

"Oh, please don't say that! I feel bad enough that you've been dragged into this again." Riley opened the fridge, pulling out an untouched slice of Junior's devil's food cheesecake and presenting it to Marco. "Please take this. I know it's your favorite and it's the least I can do."

"Thank you," he blushed, taking the container from her hands.

Marco was still awfully shy around Riley outside of the office.

He reminded Riley of herself in that way. There was the always-on-his-game Work Marco, and the reserved and awkward Regular Marco. She was sympathetic to his dual selves considering she was just the same.

The slight hint of alcohol that Riley detected off his breath now suggested that she had just stolen him from a get together with friends. Though Riley felt bad about doing so, she could see that Marco was feeling sheepish about being caught drinking in the middle of the workweek.

But considering he had never come into work hungover or unprepared, it wasn't like Riley would care.

After saying goodbye to Marco, Riley shut the door and collapsed on her couch, exhaling so hard she swore she made the windows rattle. She reached into her purse to pull out her antihistamines. Despite how tired she was, she knew she could probably use some help sleeping tonight. Riley squinted at the fine print on the back of her box.

Do not take more than one tablet in 24 hours.

She wrinkled her itchy nose. *Then why don't you last the full 24 hours?*

She stood up in anger, slamming the box down on the kitchen counter, right next to where she had left the Polaroid.

Ugh.

As angry as she was, it still looked ominous enough that she felt prickles on the back of her neck. Riley rolled her eyes at the overly dramatic nature of Evan's tactics.

"We're never really alone," she muttered, reading aloud. Heartfelt messages were never Evan's strong suit. But he sure knew his way around creeping people out.

After running into her neighbor then seeing Marco, Riley felt like she had reconnected with reality. She felt less weird about the dark figure walking behind her. The person had given no true indication that he wanted anything to do with Riley and he had just as much of a right to be on the street at night as she did.

And as quiet as it seemed in that moment, she was actually surrounded by people. She always was. That was what was great about living in the city.

It wasn't all that late, even. Sure, it was past midnight, but that didn't mean anything.

Dogs still needed to be walked, as proven by her neighbor. Young people were still out drinking late, as proven by Marco.

Riley had just managed to psych herself out. Which again, she thought was fair considering the events of the past twenty-four hours.

She walked over to her window, glancing outside. From the safety of her home, the darkness and silence of her little block appeared tranquil. Not at all foreboding, like it had been shortly before.

It was all about perspective – like everything in life.

Riley yawned, reaching for the cord to shut her blinds. She couldn't be more ready to say goodbye to this very strange day.

But then a sudden flash of light cut through the darkness.

Riley froze.

She stared out at the darkness, wondering where the flash had come from. She listened for rain. Had she just seen lightning?

It didn't appear to be raining.

Stop. You just talked yourself out of a paranoid spiral.

She pulled on the cord again, lowering the blinds another third of the way down when she saw some movement in the building across the street.

Normally, this wouldn't be unusual.

New Yorkers were quite used to observing others as well as being observed within their own apartments.

But the building across the street was vacant. A new condo still under construction.

It was far too late for construction workers to still be lurking. And they certainly wouldn't be working in the dark.

Riley lowered the shades the rest of the way, turning off her light so she could peer out undetected.

There was definitely someone in there.

A dark, hunched over figure.

A looming shadow that stared right back.

———

8

"Why'd you change your number?" Sierra asked as she watched Riley return texts on her phone.

They sat together in the backseat of an Uber, on their way to the third potential venue on their list for the day. Brighton peered into the rearview mirror from the passenger seat, looking towards Riley as if he was also interested in the answer.

"You know that guy that was in the office before you two came in that day?" Riley asked.

"Oh, yep. Say no more," Sierra shrugged her perfectly sculpted shoulders, as if she was suddenly embarrassed for asking.

Riley had felt a deep sense of relief with her new phone number. She picked a 917 area code, shedding her upstate past for good. *No more 845. No more depending on others. No more paranoia.*

She had been feeling strong and confident and particularly good about herself since making that change. And a couple days removed from the worst day ever, she was finally able to appreciate the path her new life was on. She had a brand new office, lovely new clients, and a gorgeous romantic prospect that made her feel like as much of a catch as he was.

But sitting next to Sierra was the quickest way to shake any sense of self-assuredness.

Today, Sierra was dressed in a short white dress that clung to a figure that Riley hadn't seen that first day they met. She had assumed Sierra was as willowy as she appeared in her loose-fitting dress, but it turned out she was rocking some pretty serious curves – all in the right spots.

Though Riley was petite, she was pretty curvy herself. It was the only thing she could say she had in common with her mother. But being short with curves meant that most of the cheesecake purchases she made ended up being donations to Marco. She could have the thrill of buying the food, but not the thrill of eating it. Because if she ate all the cheesecake she wanted (and she wanted all of it), her upper curves and lower curves quickly met up in the middle.

Sierra's curves not only sat on a long and lithe frame, she was also surprisingly fit. Lines of muscle ran down her long legs and arms and she was light on her feet, moving with the elegance of a ballet dancer.

Riley was so completely amazed by her that there was no room for envy.

Additionally, Sierra was so, *so* incredibly kind and friendly. She had taken to Riley immediately and was warm and affectionate in a way that didn't feel forced or uncomfortable. And she was a hugger, hugging more than your basic greeting or goodbye. She hugged every time she was thankful or excited or saw something she liked.

Brighton was standoffish in comparison, but perfectly friendly outside the context of Sierra. He wasn't as touchy-feely. His hands remained mostly in his pockets. He was quiet, but always smiling. Quietly gorgeous to his fiancée's gregariously gorgeous. And it was Riley's job to find an equally gorgeous venue that suited this gorgeous couple.

But there weren't many venues available with such short notice. Most of the popular ones had been booked months, even years in advance. The list Riley came up with were of venues that didn't normally host weddings or guest lists of over a hundred, but she hoped that they'd either find ways to accommodate Sierra and

Brighton's request or the couple would consider cutting down the guest list.

The third venue on the list was one Riley had hesitated to put on at all.

She held her breath as their car pulled up in front.

Bisset was a family-owned restaurant in a two-story Fort Greene townhouse with a garden out back. It was very modestly decorated with its cream-colored finish, walnut crown molding, and fresh wildflowers sticking out of glass vases that hung from the walls.

It was far from the most popular venue, which Riley always thought confounding. She had found its humble charm a huge draw.

And she was pretty sure she wasn't just being biased because she had had her own wedding there...

"I love this," Brighton said, running his hands over the long family table sitting in the middle of the dining room. It was the first full sentence he had spoken all day, even if it was only three words.

"Brighton is a woodworker," Sierra explained. "He's always been great with his hands." Brighton looked up, squinting at Sierra for the phrasing. She winked in return.

"I never asked what you do," Riley realized, turning to Sierra.

"I'm a..." Sierra pursed her lips, considering her words. "A general crafter, I guess is what you can call me. Although now, the bulk of my income comes from embroidery projects commissioned through Etsy."

Called it, Riley thought, smiling to herself. She had pinned them as those perfect Brooklyn couples that somehow made their living through handcrafted, bespoke items. They fit the stereotype perfectly.

"So with this venue," Sierra said, looking up the spiral stairwell that sat in the back corner, "we'd get the whole place? Like upstairs and downstairs and the garden?"

"Yes," Riley nodded. "It can definitely accommodate a hundred people, although perhaps not everyone in a single room which might affect how you want to handle the evening."

"May I peek upstairs?" Sierra asked.

"Go ahead."

"Babe, you want to come?" Sierra looked at Brighton. He was now inspecting a hand-painted sideboard boasting a collection of Limoges porcelain.

"In a second," Brighton muttered.

Oh wow, another three-word sentence, Riley smirked.

Sierra narrowed her eyes at the back of his head, pausing a second before proceeding upstairs.

Riley wandered out back into the tiny garden.

They had held their ceremony there, surrounded by the fresh tomatoes, figs, and herbs that the Bissets planted around the perimeter of the space.

Riley's mother had paid for their wedding, something she still felt kind of guilty about. Judy was over the moon to hear that Riley was getting married – mostly because it meant that there'd be someone official to "watch" over her.

Judy had hated the idea of her daughter leaving their small upstate farm town to go to school in the city because that meant Riley would be out of smothering distance. When Judy actually allowed her to go (after a week-long meltdown), Riley thought her mother did so because she had come up with a plan to move into the city with her. Judy had always been *that type* of mother. Even though the whole purpose of leaving their small town was to put some distance between them, Riley had already prepared herself for the possibility of Judy tagging along.

But to her surprise, Judy didn't budge. She said she couldn't leave the house where her husband had passed. Where she had raised her daughter. It was her first win over Judy. The very first time she was able to make a decision of her own.

The fact that Judy paid for her wedding still made her uncomfortable, the way that her finding the office space made Riley uncomfortable. It meant that she was still accepting help from her mother, despite insisting on keeping their distance.

Judy loved her. Riley recognized that. But she was just never really able to stomach the way Judy expressed it.

Riley had always heard that women instinctively sought husbands similar to their fathers. But Riley never knew her father. So instead, she picked a husband like her mother – possessive, controlling, and providing of a special brand of "care" that crippled her sense of autonomy.

But as she stood there in her wedding venue, remembering her mother proudly walking her down the aisle, she felt bad about how little she spoke with Judy these days. Riley needed the distance just so she could continue to breathe normally, to live normally. And Judy was just a constant reminder of all the things in the world that she should be afraid of, all the things she was incapable of.

The fact that Judy respected the distance now almost made her feel worse. Where once she would call the police if Riley didn't answer a text within the hour, Judy had now grown used to only hearing from Riley once every two weeks. In that phone call, they would provide each other a stoic bullet-point list of everything new in their lives.

But it had gotten difficult again since her split with Evan. Judy's worst worries were all flaring up again, Riley just knew it.

So she let herself miss their phone call this week. And to make it worse, she hadn't even informed Judy of her new number.

"Look at this trellis!"

Riley turned to see Brighton had stepped outside behind her and was now running his fingers over the latticework that held up the tomato vines.

It was the most excitement *and* the most words she had heard out of him all day.

"You *really* like woodworking, don't you?" Riley teased.

"It's my job," Brighton replied. "It's good to like your job, right?"

"Of course," Riley said. His earnestness was refreshing. She walked up behind him as he continued to study the woodwork before him.

"I think this used to be a door, you see?" He pointed his finger around the perimeter of the trellis, ending on the cut out circle where a doorknob used to be. "Yep. I thought so." He was talking to himself more than he was to Riley.

"Where'd you learn woodworking?" Riley asked.

"My grandfather," Brighton replied. "My dad wasn't interested in it growing up so he was more than happy to teach me. We mostly worked with fresh timber back then. Where we lived up in Vermont there was plenty. But here, I do mostly repurposed stuff."

"That's what's in now, right?"

"Yeah, but I do it not because it's 'in,'" he smiled. "I just think it's what's right, to reuse rather than create new waste. And repurposing is about second chances and new lives. It just feels...meaningful. And inspiring."

Riley cocked her head, studying Brighton as his attention moved from the trellis to the tomato plants it held. He reached up to touch a green one, as if punctuating his spur of the moment poetry. She felt her heart flutter. Second chances, new lives...repurposing. Making old things new. She loved the sentiment. In his simple statement, she made Riley feel like all those things were possible for her own life.

"I really like that," Riley finally said.

Brighton turned to her. Suddenly, he looked a bit embarrassed, as if he had only then realized he said everything aloud.

Then he burst out laughing.

Riley couldn't help but feel charmed. There was something alluring about his quiet energy. The fact that he rationed his words somehow made him feel all the more captivating.

And there was something in his crystal blue eyes that suggested more depth than he cared to express. Riley reminded herself that quiet people always *appeared* smarter, just because they had less chances to put their foot in their mouth.

She suddenly realized they had held their silent gaze for far too long.

Riley quickly looked away, exhaling quickly as she tugged on her earlobe to stop her fidgety hands. She blushed.

"Everything okay?" Brighton asked, furrowing his brows.

"Of course," Riley replied, nervously. She hoped he hadn't

detected the flicker of attraction she had felt. *It was* just *a flicker.* "Why do you ask that?"

"Oh, I don't know," Brighton frowned, as if suddenly wondering why he had asked that himself. "I think it's because Sierra does that when she's upset, so I just assumed...you were."

"What do I do?" Sierra asked, appearing suddenly in the doorframe.

"You know, that thing..." Brighton's voice tapered down to a much softer volume. Riley watched as whatever glimpse into his personality she had gotten retreated once again. "With your ear."

"Oh, *that* thing," Sierra replied. She turned to Riley to explain. "I tug on my ear when I'm cranky. I don't know where I picked that up."

"That's funny," Riley said. "I don't think I ever realized I even did that until Brighton pointed it out."

"Why are you cranky?"

"I'm not." Riley pursed her lips.

She really wasn't. She just felt weird being attracted to her client.

She also felt a bit strange about how quickly Brighton changed as soon as Sierra reappeared.

It reminded her of Evan – or more specifically, the way Riley was around him.

She realized she was still pulling at her ear. It took quite a bit of effort to force her hands back down to her sides. They stayed there for just a second before she opted to play with the pendant on her bracelet again.

"So what'd you think of the upstairs?" Riley asked.

"Oh my God, it's incredible," Sierra said, clutching at her heart. "I love the bay window overlooking the garden. It's so cozy and homey and absolutely everything I want."

"Really?" Riley asked, half excited, half not looking forward to having to work in what now felt like a graveyard for her marriage.

"What do you think, babe?" she asked Brighton.

He thought for a beat.

Sierra arched a shapely eyebrow, her lips pressed into a thin line as she watched her fiancé. It was as if she was surprised he had his own opinion.

Brighton caught the look. His expression quickly changed to match her initial enthusiasm.

"I love it too!" he said. "It really is perfect."

"Well, then it's settled!" Sierra exclaimed. Her limbs exploded outwards as she leaped onto her fiancé and wrapped her slender arms around his neck and her long legs around his waist.

Brighton's feigned enthusiasm quickly became something real. He lowered Sierra to the ground so he could plant a hard kiss on her mouth.

Riley smiled for them, although inside, she couldn't shake that odd feeling of déjà vu.

Evan had looked warm and friendly from the outside, but it was all a ruse.

She wondered if the same could be said for Sierra.

9

A long day of venue shopping usually ended in the comfort of her pajamas, reclined on her couch, wrapped around a tub of Trader Joe's mini chocolate chip cookies.

But today was another catch up day, and tonight, she'd be forced to cross the 9pm threshold at the office.

The urgency of Sierra and Brighton's wedding had stolen Riley's focus from her other open accounts. She was long overdue for status updates on all her other projects – what she could recall off the top of her head to be a product reveal party by a whiskey distillery in Vinegar Hill, a new hotel's employee training event in Dumbo, and a retirement party at a law firm in Brooklyn Heights.

She had asked Marco to leave the binders out on her desk for her so that she could get straight to it once she got into the office.

The building looked different at night – even more vast and empty than it did during the day. As she swiped her card in through the front door, she just about felt the emptiness in her bones. Despite the warm spring air, there was a sharp coldness inside.

The stairwell door slammed behind her, echoing just a bit louder without the usual ambient noise of distant jackhammers and table saws. The second floor was almost pitch black, but had the faintest blue-grey glow from the moonlight outside.

Riley hated that the motion sensor hall lights took its time to turn on. She certainly didn't love having to stare into the dark abyss for longer than she had to. She also took it as an affront towards her diminutive physique – as if even electronics had trouble spotting her.

She raised her hands above her head, waving her arms until one of the overhead lights began to warm up and then *click* – the entire floor was flooded with fluorescent.

Riley rushed down the hall, her keys out and ready to just get in and get out.

She raised it to the door, pressing it into the lock.

She missed the opening, causing the tiniest little spark as the key scratched the side of the lock. It was just the slightest force, but suddenly, the door creaked open.

It had been left unlocked.

It was uncharacteristic of Marco to be anything short of extremely responsible, but Riley chalked it up to the confusion of having to share a set of office keys ever since she lost her own. With the backlog of work, they hadn't had a chance to get a new copy. But she knew that continuing to pass the key back and forth was only going to create more issues.

She switched on the light and immediately noticed the binders pulled out on her desk, like she had asked for. But rather than lined neatly side by side, like Marco always made sure to do, the binders were laid out crooked with its pages flipped open haphazardly.

Riley made a beeline towards the desk. *Dear lord, was Marco drunk or something?*

They had always shared a strong dislike for dog-eared pages. It was, embarrassingly, a key factor to why Riley hired him over another perfectly qualified candidate in the first place.

What was he thinking leaving everything out all sloppy like that?

She lowered herself into her white leather Herman Miller chair, spinning it to face her desk.

Each binder was opened to the itinerary for the date of each event.

A restrained exhale crept out from between her lips.

From the opposite corner, someone exhaled back.

Riley gasped, jumping to her feet.

It wasn't paranoia this time.

Right in the spot she had seem him last stood Evan.

"You blocked my number again," he said, matter-of-factly. As if it was totally normal for him to be there.

No, I changed my number, Riley thought. But she wasn't about to tell him that.

"How'd you get in here?" she asked. *Oh my God, he must've taken my keys that day...*

"You forced me out of my own home by making me seem like some kind of monster," Evan spat, ignoring her question. "When in reality, you were the one who made me this way."

Riley gripped her phone in her hand, trying to sneak in a dial to 911. She wanted to appear casual, like she wasn't afraid. She didn't want to tip him off to what she was doing.

But Evan spotted it right away.

He lunged towards her, striking her arms so hard that her phone fell from her hands and skidded across the floor.

Riley gasped, her forearms stinging from the impact. She ran towards the phone, but he had grabbed hold of her, spinning her around.

She looked up at Evan in shock.

She had truly believed it when she said that she didn't think Evan would lay a hand on her, no matter how bad he got. Did this really just happen? Did it count? *This has to count.* She felt the pain radiating through her arms. This counted. This definitely counted.

"Oh my God," she whispered. *Oh my God.*

Oh my God.

Riley was alone with a madman in her empty office building on the quietest possible corner of an already quiet neighborhood.

And she didn't know *this* Evan.

She didn't know how to predict his next move, react to him. She had no idea this was even underneath the man she *thought* she had figured out over the last decade.

How could this be? How could she get someone so wrong?

Evan wrapped his hands around her upper arms, holding her so tight she could already feel the inevitable bruises.

"You're hurting me," she whispered. Her voice warbled. She sounded weak. She looked up at the unrecognizable expression on Evan's face. *How could you be this stupid? How could you not know he was capable of this?*

He's going to kill me.

Oh my God, he's going to kill me.

"Are you ready to listen to me?" he bellowed. There was vodka on his breath. His eyes were tearing, red. What had he been doing?

"Yes! Yes, of course," Riley sputtered. She tried to force a smile for him. Maybe that could calm him? If she looked friendly? She must've looked maniacal. She sure felt it. "Let's talk. Let's talk now, I'm listening."

Riley watched Evan's eyes track the tear she could feel rolling down her cheek.

She felt faint. She felt out of body. She felt her vision brown out.

Then, she felt a second pair of hands grab her by the waist and suddenly, Evan's body flew backwards.

He landed hard on the ground as he clutched his stomach.

"Are you okay?" a gruff voice asked.

Gabriel.

"I don't know," Riley answered, still in shock. She felt Gabriel push her back as he lunged for Evan again, grabbing him by the front of his shirt.

"Who the hell are you?" Evan yelled, pulling at Gabriel's arms in vain. Riley realized he was struggling to get his feet firmly on the ground as Gabriel dragged him towards the front door.

"You're trespassing," Gabriel bellowed. "Would you like me to call the cops?"

"What, so I can report you for assault?" Evan sneered. Gabriel tugged his shirt upwards, pulling Evan into an even more awkward position. He flailed, his face turning red.

"I'm giving you a choice, which I think is very generous of me," Gabriel said, coolly. "I can call the cops and you'll wait here to be arrested. Or you can fuck off forever and if I ever see you near Riley again, assault will be the least of your worries."

"You don't scare me," Evan sputtered. It was a struggle for him to say even that much.

"If you were smart, I really should." Gabriel let go of Evan's shirt, letting him crumple to the ground.

Evan pushed himself up, making a line drive into Gabriel's torso.

With just one hand, Gabriel blocked Evan's efforts. Then he grabbed him by the crick of his neck and dragged him out like an oversized rag doll.

10

A fter catching her breath, Riley ran out after Gabriel and
Evan. She was surprised to find the hallway already empty
– and then the stairwell. They had somehow already
managed to leave the building.

She sped up, worried over what she was about to witness outside.

Evan had just done what Riley never thought he could do. He had
struck her, restrained her.

And now Gabriel was maybe going to kill him?

As awful as everything had been, she didn't want Gabriel to kill
Evan, for all of their sakes. It would be a bad end for all of them.

Out on the sidewalk, the night air felt biting and the slight breeze
had carried the canal's infamous odor onto their block. Gabriel held
Evan by the forearms the way Evan had held her earlier.

Now, finally, Evan appeared scared.

Riley ran towards them, her heels clicking furiously. Neither of
them looked over.

In the moonlight, the glint of something hanging from Evan's belt
caught her eye.

Her keys.

He had taken them after all.

"Give them back," Gabriel commanded as Riley approached.

With his motion still limited, Evan obeyed, reaching into his pocket carefully and handing the keys over to Riley.

"There are cameras in the building that have recorded you trespassing, do you understand that?" Gabriel asked.

"She wouldn't have that office if it weren't for me," Evan said.

"Sounds like you can't handle her having something you can't touch."

"Please," Evan scoffed. He turned just slightly towards Riley. "Half that business is mine. I supported you while you were building it. If you were to divorce me, you'd owe that much to me. Keep that in mind."

Riley stayed quiet. She wasn't sure if that was true. The lawyer she had contacted had been solely focused on getting Evan to sign the papers at all.

"She started the business before you were even married," Gabriel said. "She only got the *office* after. So you're wrong. You're not getting anything."

Riley cocked her head. *I never told him that.*

She backed up just a bit.

I know I never told him that.

Suddenly, Gabriel let go of Evan so forcefully he stumbled off the curb and into the street. He regained his footing just in time to stay on the sidewalk.

"You should go," Gabriel said to him. "You know, while I'm still feeling generous."

Evan was still fuming, but he knew he had been defeated.

After one more scathing glare at Riley, he turned and walked off.

11

Riley kept quiet about Gabriel's little slip up.

It was clear to her now that he *was* a creep, but she hadn't figured out to what extent. And she wanted to.

How did he know she had started the business before she married Evan? Sure, it was public record, *somewhere*, but why would he even look it up to begin with?

And better yet, how did he know to come upstairs when he did? Could he hear through the vents what was going on in her office? Or was he...just there? For reasons that Riley couldn't figure out?

After thanking him profusely for what good he *did* do (creep or not, he *had* saved her), she accepted Gabriel's offer to go to a 24-hour diner a few blocks over. She retrieved her phone and her binders and stuck it all in a tote, and even let Gabriel carry them for her as they walked there.

Riley thought maybe that appearing unsuspicious would be the best way to assure she'd be safe until they got somewhere more populated.

Because now it was clear Gabriel was as two-faced as everyone else around her.

In the diner, she tried to remain chatty and casual, flashing the occasional smile as they ordered milkshakes and a plate of mozzarella sticks and disco fries to share.

Riley looked around. There were at least two servers, a cook, and a manager on duty. At the window booth was a pair of off-duty but uniformed policemen on a second round of coffee.

Feeling safely surrounded, she knew then that she couldn't hold her question for another second. So Riley blurted it out.

"How did you know when I started my company?" she asked. Her voice sounded alien to her. Threatening.

"You told me," Gabriel answered, furrowing his brows.

"No," Riley shook her head. "No, I didn't."

"There's no other way I'd know," he frowned.

"I've been admittedly a little...off lately, but I know for a fact that I didn't tell you when I started my company and now I need to know why you felt the need to look it up."

"Alright," Gabriel sighed. "I mean, I look up everyone I date. Don't you? Isn't that just what people do now?"

"Facebook, I get. Any social media, I get. But you dug so deep that you found New York State's records of when I started my LLC? Really?" Riley blinked. *Oh my God.* Another thing struck her. She was pretty sure she hadn't even told Gabriel how long she and Evan had been married. This was worse than she thought. "What are you? Are you a cop? Private investigator? Why do you know so much about me? Who sent you?"

The server sidled up beside their booth, smiling wide as he set down their milkshakes. Riley watched as Gabriel's eyes flicked back and forth, as if trying to figure out how to back out of their situation. She had him cornered now.

Finally, he exhaled, leaning back against the booth as he ran a hand over the stubble accumulating on his jawline.

"Okay. I'm sorry," he began. "I didn't really want to do any of this at all."

Riley's heart pounded hard against her chest. Her pulse flared up everywhere it knew to – her temples, her wrists, her throat. She even felt it in her forearms and biceps where Evan had made contact.

"So you *were* stalking me?" Riley hissed. "You *were* following me? You *lied* to me. Who are you, even? Do you even work in the studio downstairs? Or was that some made up story to explain why you're always so conveniently nearby?"

"I work downstairs. I own that company. That's not a lie."

"Well, who *else* do you work for?" Riley raised her eyebrows along with her volume. Her voice cracked. She couldn't believe what was happening. She felt like some hardened interrogator on one of those police procedurals. "Is it Evan? Did Evan send you? Was all that just for show before?"

"No, Jesus, of course not," Gabriel replied. "It's not Evan." He heaved a thundering sigh, looking just as distressed as she did now. He couldn't even make eye contact.

"Then who is it?"

"It's..." He hesitated. For a moment, Riley could see him trying to come up with another lie. But then the stress in his eyes suddenly dropped away. He was resolved now. Gabriel looked up, catching Riley's gaze as he regained his grounds. "It's Judy. Your mother."

12

The stress and sleep had caught up to Riley in the ugliest manner.

She knew she looked like hell and she *really* preferred not to look like hell when meeting up with Judy since Judy would *definitely* have something to say about it.

But she couldn't even bring herself to care about that now. Not when Judy had sent a *spy* to keep tabs on her.

God.

She could feel herself tearing up. Not just for the betrayal, but because she had momentarily believed a man like Gabriel might actually be interested in her.

How embarrassing.

She had run from the diner as soon as Gabriel revealed that Judy was involved. Left him with her full glass of milkshake and the bill. Riley didn't care. She just wanted to get away from him. She'd let him pay for everything this time – because she wanted him to pay in *some* form for what he had done.

Riley looked out the window of her car, blinking back tears.

Judy was just so good at this. In her efforts to help Riley, she always did so much more harm than whatever aid she was hoping to provide.

And suddenly, memories of her tenth birthday flickered in her mind.

Ten was a big deal. She had entered double digits. And Judy wanted to throw her the party of a lifetime.

But Riley didn't want that. Because Riley didn't have friends. And you needed friends to have guests at your birthday.

Judy went ahead anyway, surprising Riley with an extravagant birthday party at a Victorian teahouse on the Hudson. All the girls from her grade were there, clothed in frilly dresses of satin and tulle, seated around little tables with three-tier platters of scones and tea sandwiches.

And they were *actually* excited to see her.

Riley was thrilled. And for six years after, that birthday was marked as the best day of her life.

That was until her high school "best friend" Jennifer revealed that they had all been bribed. Parents included.

Like the guests at her tenth birthday party, Gabriel wasn't real. Gabriel was someone sent by Judy to monitor and control Riley's life. Another humiliating and horrifying example of Judy's meddling.

The Uber stopped in front of a beautiful Carroll Gardens townhouse.

Riley thanked the driver and stepped out.

She was at the address that Judy had provided when Riley had finally gotten in touch with her. To her surprise, Judy was in the city visiting a friend and insisted Riley go to her rather than the other way around. She knew this was another one of Judy's tactics to temper her behavior. She assumed Riley would be less likely to explode in the presence of whoever this friend of Judy's was.

Riley sure hoped Judy's mysterious friend was ready to get the earful she was about to give her mother.

When the front door opened, it wasn't Judy greeting her on the other side.

It wasn't even anyone Riley would suspect could actually *be* a friend of Judy's.

Gabriel stood in the doorframe, practically filling it, looking at Riley in a sheepish manner.

"What's going on?" Riley asked. "What is this?"

"This is my house."

"You're my mother's friend?" Riley furrowed her brows in disgust. "Please tell me this isn't some sort of Mrs. Robinson thing."

"Jesus, Riley!" Gabriel's expression matched hers now. "Just come in, she's inside."

Riley followed, more confused than ever.

As she did, she marveled at the beauty of the townhouse's interior.

It was old-fashioned with its hardwood floors, crown molding, and the occasional stain-glassed panels trimming the windows. The ornate décor of gold-framed oil paintings, grandfather clocks, and porcelain figurines didn't look like anything a thirty-five year old man would readily choose.

Riley wondered for a second if Gabriel was a professional sugar baby. Or a gigolo. One of those gorgeous men that got paid to accompany rich old ladies. Maybe Judy thought it was more economic to hire someone like him rather than an actual private investigator.

Gabriel led Riley to a back parlor facing a small, well-kept backyard.

Judy sat in the window seat, looking as regal as she always did. Her grey hair was cut short with the exception of a longer, stylish swoop of waves that hung over her forehead. She wore a billowy white blouse tucked into navy slacks.

For a woman of seventy-one, Judy could still pass for someone twenty years younger. She was as stately and beautiful as Riley always remembered her to be. The impossible standard she knew she'd never reach. Preserved forever at the prime of her life.

The same couldn't be said for the woman sitting beside her.

Riley recognized the woman to be Margaret, one of Judy's friends from their town upstate. She used to be a frequent visitor – a jolly ball of fun and goofiness that Riley always looked forward to seeing. Margaret's hair was a different color every time she visited – and it was never a color that occurred naturally in humans. As a child, Margaret seemed like the coolest adult alive.

It never made any sense to her that Margaret could be friends with someone as stoic and serious as Judy was, but she had noticed that her mother was always a little more relaxed and eager to enjoy herself in her best friend's presence.

It had been thirteen years since Riley had seen Margaret, and she was looking nothing like she used to. Her wild-colored hair was just white now. There was no jolliness or fun or goofiness left in her shriveled frame.

Margaret sat like a shell of her former self, staring out into space as Judy held her hand.

Riley felt gut-punched.

Judy definitely did this on purpose. She knew Riley wouldn't dare tear into her in the presence of Margaret looking the way she did.

What a manipulative move.

It was surprising still because Judy wasn't really the manipulative type. She was smothering, overbearing, overwhelming, and meddling, but she had always been straightforward about her actions. Manipulative was Evan's thing.

But then again, Judy had hired someone to spy on her. She had *him* do the lying and manipulating for her. That still counted, right?

Maybe she was being unfair...maybe she was over-interpreting it all in her anger. Maybe she owed Judy a chance to explain. Did that mean she owed Evan a chance to explain?

No. God, no.

But she didn't really know anymore. She felt like she didn't know anything anymore.

All she knew now was that she was standing next to a man she had once thought was a date and looking at a very sad Judy with a very frail Margaret.

"Riley," Judy said, tilting her head as she gazed at her daughter.

She let go of Margaret's hand and held her arms out. "Riley sweet-heart, I'm so sorry."

Riley stood unmoving.

Judy got up, embracing her tight. She rested her pointy chin atop Riley's head, as she always did when hugging her. Though she couldn't see Judy's face, she knew her mother was crying.

"I'm so, *so* sorry," she repeated. "I was wrong. I was just desperate. When I heard you two were working in the same building, I just asked him to check up on you if he could, that's all. I didn't mean to make this into such a mess."

Riley couldn't bring herself to hug her mother back.

She was surprised by how remorseful Judy was. That was definitely not what she had prepared for. Riley had geared up to fight and scream about how she was sick of Judy violating her privacy and treating her like some defenseless child. She was planning on shaming Judy for hiring a potentially dangerous stranger to learn about Riley's life. She wanted Judy to know that her actions of concern were more detrimental than helpful.

But it seemed now that Gabriel wasn't hired at all.

She was pretty sure she had figured it out now.

Gabriel must've been one of Margaret's sons.

Riley had never met any of Margaret's kids because they were a bit older and they were boys – nothing she was interested in as a child. But she remembered hearing about them and how insane her household was with all the giant men lumbering about.

Riley found it in her to raise her arms, patting Judy gently on the back. It was the most she could muster up in her confusion.

The gesture was what made Judy finally back away. She held Riley at an arm's length, gazing at her with that sickly amount of love that she was never able to accept.

"I haven't seen you in ages," Judy said. Riley braced herself for the dramatic concern over her ragged appearance. The last time Judy had seen Riley was Christmas, when she was admittedly still somewhat well-adjusted to her life and not stuck in a whirlwind of traumatic changes.

But Judy didn't say anything. Instead, she let go of Riley quickly, as if she suddenly realized she had exceeded the quota of affection that Riley could handle. She backed up again, sitting beside Margaret who remained staring into space as she had before.

"This was my parents' place before they moved upstate," Gabriel explained, gesturing for Riley to take a seat on a tufted bench along the wall across from their mothers. She sat down, too surprised still to protest. "I took over the deed when the last renters moved out then moved in when I got back to the states. Then I moved my mom down when my dad passed away, so I can take care of her. So we've been roommates for a year."

Riley then realized what this meant for Judy. Her only real friend had left town. There was no one left up there for her mother. She was even more alone now than she'd ever been.

"She's gotten worse since Teddy died," Judy explained. "I come down every once in awhile to say hello."

"I usually call Judy when my mom's having a good day," Gabriel continued. "It gets kind of extreme now. There are days where she can even call Judy on her own and then days where she's like this."

"We had a good day yesterday when I first got in." Judy took Margaret's hands into hers again. "She was chatty and we even painted together like we used to."

"So..." Riley whispered. Her voice was hoarse. "You take care of Margaret on your own?" She looked up at Gabriel, whose eyes were still on his mother. He was smiling at her in a way Riley had never smiled for Judy.

"We have an aid for when I'm working," Gabriel said. "And Judy helps too."

"I'm barely ever here," Judy chuckled. Her eyes gleamed, flattered and proud. "Gabriel just doesn't like admitting that he's a saint."

"I'm no saint," Gabriel said. "Far from it. I just want to be here for my mom because, well, she's my mom and she's wonderful. Even if her brand of parenting fostered a deep anxiety that I still suffer from today." He smirked at his own joke.

"We parents never know what we're doing," Judy laughed

awkwardly. She had on a stiff smile and her eyes were fixed on the ground.

"So," Gabriel said, clapping his hands together. "I'm craving ramen. How about you, Judy? You want some of that spicy miso we got last time?"

"Oh!" Judy perked up. "Yes, I would!"

"Alright then!" Gabriel replied. He looked over at Riley, tilting his head towards the front door. "You. Come help me carry some takeout."

13

"I should've just told you upfront that I knew Judy."

Gabriel and Riley sat at the counter of the ramen shop, waiting for their orders. Clouds of fragrant steam rolled through the air between them. Riley kept her eyes fixed on the chefs working, still unsure of how to handle all that she knew now.

"Especially after you said everything about your relationship with her," Gabriel continued.

"Did she tell you not to tell me?"

"She said not to tell you that I was asked to look out for you," he explained. "But she didn't say I couldn't tell you that we knew each other."

"So why didn't you?"

"The first time we met, I recognized you from the photo Judy showed me," Gabriel said. "The only thing was in real life, you were a whole lot cuter than I expected."

"Because I'm small?" Riley scoffed.

"Because you're hot."

"Oh," she blushed.

"So I didn't mention it because I thought it'd hurt my chances for a date."

"I see."

"Which was dumb. And for sure creepy. I see that now."

"When you said you grew up in New York, I thought you meant the city."

"Nope. We grew up in a town right next to yours. Judy actually said she and your dad moved up because of my parents."

"Really?" Riley found that surprising. Judy seemed like she'd be the one who moved out of the city and convinced her much more outgoing best friend to join her.

"Yeah, they were really close," Gabriel nodded. "I mean, they still are when my mom's like, you know, normal." Riley scrambled to say something comforting, but she noticed that Gabriel's attention wasn't even entirely on the words he was saying. His eyes were fixed on their food as the chef packed up their first order.

"I'm sorry my mom got you involved in this mess," she said, finally. She meant it. Gabriel didn't know Judy the way Riley knew Judy. So how was he to know that this would happen?

"Nah, it was my fault how this played out," Gabriel shrugged. "I was the one who told her that my brother gave me a spot in his building for my business and she mentioned that you'd be moving in and that we should perhaps meet up. But then she never followed up on that. But then she got *really* worried about you after Evan split and asked that I make sure you were okay. It was all very vague on her end. I'm the one who messed it up by using her concern as a dating service."

Ohh...

Gabriel's brother was the owner of their building. It made a whole lot more sense that all of Judy's city connections belonged to a single family.

"Alright," Riley smiled. "I get it."

"She means well," Gabriel said.

"I mean, sure," Riley shrugged. "But good intentions don't always have good outcomes."

"Yeah, don't I know that now," Gabriel laughed. "Listen, I'm sorry again. Really. For everything. I'm sorry to *and* for Judy as well. I didn't mean to drive the wedge further. That was the last thing I wanted to do."

"And I'm sorry I thought you were some shady gigolo my mother hired to be a janky P.I."

"*What?*" Gabriel's jaw dropped. "*That's* what you thought was happening? Jesus, no wonder you were so upset." Riley laughed, finally feeling her muscles relax a little. She almost felt like she was on that date with Gabriel again.

"I have one more question," she asked. "How'd you know Evan was in my office? How'd you know something was wrong?"

"I heard you," Gabriel replied. "All my students were gone and I was closing up shop so it was quiet and the vents we share are like those cup and string telephones we made in elementary school. I can hear stuff from my end too. But only when there isn't a class in session"

"Did you tell my mom about any of that?" she asked. "About how we went on a date? Or Evan breaking in?"

"Of course not," Gabriel scoffed. "I'm not about to scare her like that."

"I think she'd *like* the part about us dating."

"That part I didn't tell her because I wasn't sure where we stood," Gabriel smiled. "Didn't want to get her hopes up. She loves me, you know. I'm pre-vetted."

"You understand that the fact that you're so close to my mom is a *huge* disadvantage for you."

"Yeah, I figured," he said, frowning in an exaggerated manner. He leaned back just a bit, drumming on his belly. A silly grin spread across his face. "Oh well. I tried."

14

Riley's dreams were always vivid, which didn't bode well for her when she was having nightmares.

She already knew there was no hope for her having a normal night of sleep. Not after all these sudden revelations. But she hadn't expected to doze off into that weird mid-slumber purgatory where she was both dreaming and somehow semi-conscious.

Everything she had learned about Gabriel and Judy and Margaret was unsettling. Every single aspect of it. She felt tortured thinking about Judy being alone upstate, isolated from everyone she knew. She thought about what a wonderful son Gabriel was and how Riley would never be able to do that for Judy should she need her to.

Riley also felt ashamed over Gabriel bearing witness to what an awful daughter she actually was. Maybe it was selfish for her to be so low contact with Judy. But oftentimes, it felt like that was the only way she knew how to survive.

Finally, after an entire life under the oppressive grasp of her mother, the stress of college, and then her husband, Riley was able to live on her own terms. And she could do that if it weren't for the entire world working against her.

In her semi-lucid sleep, she recognized that whatever state of consciousness she was in would not be the restorative type. Riley was just desperate to get one single night of proper rest so she could be on her game for her meeting with Brighton and Sierra the following day. She was determined to keep her business and personal life as segregated as it used to be, but it had been difficult considering her relationship with the couple started with them witnessing the catalyst to the most challenging and confounding weeks of her life.

But she could still change things from here on out. She didn't have to bring in her grouchy, exhausted stinkface to work and subject her clients to the aftershocks of her complicated personal life.

Things always worked best that way.

Riley was still dreaming, even as her body tried to awaken.

She could see fuzzy images of familiar objects and faces, snapshots of memories taken from random parts of her mind. Like her chopsticks twirling ramen earlier that day. Gabriel's forearms. Margaret's old magenta hair. Margaret's white hair. Milkshakes. Cheesecake. Evan's gritted teeth. Her phone hitting the floor.

A loud crack rang out in her head, syncing with the image of her phone as it crashed.

She could feel her body flinch.

Another loud crack and her eyes shot open.

Riley sat up, thankful to be a hundred percent awake now. There was nothing particularly scary about what she was seeing, but it was uncomfortable to be in the in-between state for as long as she was.

CRACK.

Again.

Riley froze.

The sound was coming from outside her bedroom door.

She grabbed hold of the five-pound dumbbell she kept under her bed. Dust had collected on the rubber coating. It had been awhile since she had cleaned and even longer since she last worked out.

Riley gripped the dumbbell hard, clutching it to her chest.

Before she could change her mind, she swung open her bedroom door and switched on the lights in the living room. She held her breath, which only made her heart rate shoot up that much higher.

She did a quick look around, her eyes darting about so sharply she could feel the tug behind them.

Her living room and open kitchen were contained in a simple square, like many city apartments. There weren't many nooks and crannies because there simply wasn't the space for it. It was certainly convenient in situations like this one, where a single vantage point allowed Riley to survey the whole situation.

There was no one there, as far as she could see. Nothing seemed out of place. Nothing had been knocked over or fallen, which Riley actually hoped for because then she'd have some sort of physical explanation for the sound.

But there *was* something off.

She couldn't pinpoint it quite yet, but she knew it was there.

It was just one of those things you sensed when you'd known a space for so long. Kind of like those puzzles that she did as a kid where two near-identical photos sat side by side and you were tasked to find the subtle differences. Riley was always just a tad bit slower than her classmates in spotting all the items, but when she saw them, she would usually see them all at once.

Just like she did now.

It jumped out at her like a big red marquis arrow had suddenly lit up and pointed it out.

The lock on her front door stood vertically in the unlock position. The chain lock was unchained and swayed ever so slightly. It wasn't even cut. Just unchained. Just slid off the bar, undamaged.

How on earth...?

Riley dropped the dumbbell, running towards the door to lock and chain it once again. She grabbed the chair that sat next to her shoe rack and stuck it underneath the doorknob.

Then, she called the police.

15

"If they didn't take anything, there's nothing we can really do."

Officer Thomas was a young woman, much younger than Riley was. At least a decade. Far too young to be talking to Riley like she was a kid. *I didn't even realize children were allowed to be police now.*

Her partner, Officer Lee, was still circling the apartment, looking for "anything out of place," as if he'd even know.

"Are you *sure* you didn't leave the door unlocked," Officer Lee declared more than asked.

"Yes, I'm sure," Riley replied. "I wouldn't call you if I wasn't sure. You have to understand, I think it was my husband. He's been acting really different – like in a bad way. And it's a little more than concerning. He broke into my office the other day and he tried to restrain me."

Officer Thomas looked more concerned now. She scribbled something into her notepad.

"Did you file a report?" she asked, not looking up.

"Uh...no," Riley frowned. *God, why didn't I?* She really should have. But she was too distracted by Gabriel's whole reveal that night.

"But listen, he stole my keys from the office. I took them back, but I think he may have made a copy to come back in."

"You can file a report with me now, if you'd like," the officer said. She almost sounded bored. "Tell me what happened that night."

Riley recounted the night as best she could, ending with the fact that Gabriel had stopped Evan from doing any more harm.

But she had no evidence to provide.

Surprisingly, there were no visible bruises on Riley's arms. The security cameras in the building were only in the halls and not in the office itself. It would only show that Evan had let himself in with keys in his possession, which he could easily explain away since they were still married and it wouldn't be unheard of that her husband might have keys to the office.

All the video would show was Gabriel forcefully dragging Evan out. Violently. Which could get Gabriel in trouble.

Knowing Evan, he would concoct some story about how Riley was cheating with Gabriel and he was some jealous lover who couldn't handle the fact that Evan wouldn't grant Riley the divorce.

"Alright, ma'am," Officer Thomas said, her voice indicating that they were concluding their session, whether or not Riley was ready to. "I'm sorry we couldn't do more for you today. If you feel you are in any sort of danger here, we highly suggest that you stay somewhere else tonight. Definitely change your locks. And if your husband trespasses or becomes physical with you again, you let us know right away."

Great, Riley thought. *I have to wait to be terrorized again before I can even do anything.*

She opened the front door to let the officers out.

In the hallway, she could hear her neighbors stirring in their apartments.

It was officially morning.

16

R iley sat in her office, head buried in her hands as she sat behind her desk.

After the police left, she had gotten dressed and headed for the office, knowing full well she would not be going back to sleep.

The apartment felt like an active threat to her now.

She cursed herself for forgetting to show the officer the photo of her front door that Evan had taken. That cryptic note he had left.

That was evidence.

She could've shown them that.

But it all seemed kind of kooky. Like something she could be accused of creating herself. For attention or something. Like one of those crazy people who make drama in their own lives because they're bored.

She wanted to tell them about the fact that she felt like she was being followed, that someone was perhaps watching her from across the street. But the more she ran these lines in her head, the more Riley realized that she *did* in fact sound completely insane. That perhaps Evan was not the only one unhinged.

Where the apartment felt like an active threat, the office wasn't a whole lot better. The only thing that was of comfort to her was knowing that Gabriel was nearby. She was in no place to be denying his help, as much as she wanted to.

She had just about dozed off when Marco finally came in, surprised to see she had beaten him there. He presented her with her coffee and breakfast sandwich, then watched her with concern from his own desk, as if afraid to ask her what was wrong.

He could probably guess.

Everyone could guess, looking at her worn out face. Her exhausted body.

She wanted to tell Marco about everything that had happened. Riley wanted to talk to anyone, *anyone* that was not a part of this shit-show. Just to vent. Just to get a third party opinion.

Just so someone, *somewhere* could hold onto her story should something more happen.

But she had vowed to keep work life and personal stuff separate, and Marco was work life. He had already seen too much.

God, did Riley wish she had kept *any* of her friends from college.

Mindy was her freshman and sophomore year roommate and the only true friend she ever had. She was the *only* friend Riley had ever made on her own (if you didn't count the fact that they were randomly assigned by the university). Everyone before that was apparently bribed by Judy and everyone after was either introduced by Mindy or Evan.

In fact, her relationship with Evan was all Mindy's doing. He was her study buddy and Mindy spotted sparks the first day she brought him back to their dorm. It took forever for the two of them to finally get together, but when they did, Evan made a concerted effort to edge Mindy out. By the time it was graduation, Riley barely spoke to Mindy. And despite the fact that she had introduced them, Mindy never ended up getting an invitation to their wedding.

The friends she met through Mindy obviously sided with Mindy, and so Riley lost her lot of friends and became completely dependent on Evan's.

And when they split, she lost that lot to him too.

A knock on the door shook Riley from her stupor. For a second, it struck fear in her heart – like her body had been trained to be nothing but on alert and afraid these days.

Marco answered the door, letting in Brighton.

A light scent of patchouli and sandalwood entered with him.

He was dressed like he had just come from work in his light-weight, light blue flannel-print shirt with the sleeves rolled up to show off his toned forearms. Hints of sawdust on his jeans proved that to be true.

Brighton's beard had grown in just a bit more, making him look scruffier and more rugged than usual. When he spotted Riley, he lit up, like he was seeing an old friend.

"Hey," Riley greeted him, picking up their binder as she walked towards him. She peeked out the open door down the hall. "Where's Sierra?"

"She's not coming today," he replied. Riley cocked her head.

"How come?"

"She just had something she needed to do."

"We could've rescheduled," Riley frowned. "Today's an important day. She should be here to help make decisions." They were scheduled to sample food at Bisset's today so they could put together a menu.

"She didn't want to trouble you," Brighton shrugged. "Just because the schedule is already pretty tight. She trusts me to know her taste."

"Okay, then." Riley nodded. It was unusual for the bride not to want to be involved in something as important as the menu, but she had also noticed that couples getting married in their thirties seemed a lot more casual about the affair than those who were younger.

And Brighton sure seemed whipped enough to make the right decisions for the both of them.

17

B righton took the tasting quite seriously, taking notes in a small notebook between each bite of the chateaubriand, chicken fricassee, and salmon rillettes that Adeline Bisset presented him.

Adeline seemed oddly delighted by Brighton's careful consideration of all her cooking, peeking over his shoulder to read everything he had written. Whatever it was seemed to please her.

Riley watched from across that long family dining table that had so impressed Brighton that first day she had taken them to the location. She had happily sampled the food along with him as everything came out, relieved that he was content with her barebones level of participation. Couples normally liked to bounce their thoughts off of each other before asking Riley her opinion as well. Brighton seemed fine doing everything solo.

In fact, Riley couldn't help but notice again that he was markedly different without Sierra by his side. He was chattier. Smiled more. He just seemed more present – more willing to engaged.

She wondered if Brighton was more apt to flourish in solitude, like she suspected of herself. When Sierra was around, it seemed like everything was deferred to her. On his own, a personality would emerge and opinions were expressed.

But she could just be projecting.

With only one person at the helm, Riley was surprised how quickly they were done with their tasting. She had heard from other wedding planners that when both halves of the couple were present (and sometimes even mothers, mother-in-laws, maids of honors, and best men), decisions were made and changed at least a dozen times before anything could be settled.

But Brighton, all on his own, was in and out just like that.

"I had you scheduled in for a whole other hour so I don't know what to do with myself now," Riley joked as they stood waiting for their Uber back to the office.

"I thought it would take longer too," Brighton shrugged. "But that food was so good that I know there wasn't really a wrong decision."

"So are you heading back to work now?" she asked. "I figured that's where you were coming from before."

"Yeah," Brighton replied. "Sawdust tipped you off, right? Sorry about that. Sierra hates that I track it all over the place."

"No, it's fine," Riley laughed. "I was just curious. Where exactly do you work?"

"Right near you, actually," he said. "Just a few blocks away. Sierra and I rent a studio together."

"So you guys work in the same place and live in the same place?" Riley raised an eyebrow. "That's a lot of time together."

"Yeah, well," Brighton smiled. "It's a good thing we like each other."

"I'd hope so, since you're getting married," she teased.

An awkward, delayed smile broke across Brighton's face. Riley immediately regretted her joke. It felt as if she had brought something strange to the surface. But again, she reminded herself that she was projecting. Yes, she saw herself in Brighton. In the way his personality was suppressed in the presence of his significant other. In the way he only seemed comfortable expressing himself fully when that person wasn't in the room. It was difficult for her not to wonder if he was quietly suffering from what she had dealt with for years – because she often wished someone had seen through Evan's smoke and mirrors when she couldn't, and saved her from all that time he took away from her.

So if Riley could prevent someone from making the same mistake she did, she would do it.

But it would also put her out of a job. One that paid a very handsome and needed fee.

In the car, curiosity got the best of her.

"How's the guest list coming along?" Riley asked. She figured that was a fair question to ask considering it directly correlated with the work she was doing for them. But her intentions weren't purely professional.

"It's good," Brighton replied. "We might not actually hit a hundred invitations, though. So it might be smaller than we expected."

"Because of the short notice, you think?" The question was meant to prompt the true reason, what Riley suspected was the isolation a possessive partner might impart on their helpless significant other. Riley's own guest list was small – not even half as many people as Sierra and Brighton had intended to have. If she had to be honest with herself, Riley's only true guest was her mother. Everyone else was really there for Evan.

"No, that's not it." Brighton turned to face her. "I think maybe we just don't have a whole lot of family or friends in the area."

"Oh, really?" Riley arched an eyebrow. "Are you guys originally from somewhere else...or...?" *This isn't prying, right? These are normal questions that a normal wedding planner might ask.*

"We moved here from Austin where we met," Brighton explained. "My family's still in Vermont and they're getting older and I just wanted to be closer. And Sierra was ready to try a new city. Brooklyn seemed like the right place for us so we moved here about six months ago."

"Oh, that's not very long ago at all." Riley was surprised they wanted to plan a wedding when they were barely settled in. Especially when most of their friends were somewhere else and had barely any notice to take off work and join them.

"Sierra's been eager to just, I don't know, start over," Brighton said. He spoke half to himself again, the way he had when he was waxing poetic about woodworking.

"How come?" *Okay, now* this *is prying.* Brighton didn't seem to notice.

"She just gets antsy when she stays in one place for too long. And you know, the whole thing about starting a family closer to our own family."

"Where's her family from?"

"Actually..." Brighton bit back his lip, as if he had said something wrong. He considered something quietly before speaking again. "Sierra doesn't have any family left, so the move up here was mostly to be near mine. She wanted our kids to have access to grandparents since she never had that. Vermont was too remote for her but she was originally from New York and since it had trains up to Vermont, we figured this was our best choice."

"And how are you doing making friends up here?" Riley couldn't stop herself from the questions anymore. She was getting somewhere. Besides, Brighton didn't seem to mind them or find them invasive at all.

"A lot of my friends from Vermont are down here, actually. And it's funny, but Brooklyn woodworkers find each other so we all hang out. I don't know why I said that we don't have much friends, we actually do." Brighton looked skyward, like he was pondering his own choice of words. "I guess it's more that Sierra doesn't."

"Really?" Riley practically exclaimed. *That* was a surprise. Considering their personalities, she had been convinced it was the other way around.

"Wait, I didn't mean it like that," Brighton said, eyes wide with worry. "She has friends, just not like, you know. Enough to fill a guest list of a hundred."

"Oh, of course, that's totally normal," Riley said, waving a hand in front of her and trying to make it all seem totally casual. Who was she to judge a lack of friends? Riley was still surprised though. But then again, six months wasn't really enough time to establish close friendships.

She frowned. She kind of felt bad for judging Sierra unfairly. And so erroneously, too. Which means she *was* projecting. Brighton and Riley weren't the ones with something in common. It was Riley and Sierra.

Since they both didn't have any friends.

At least Sierra has an excuse.

"Hey, are you hungry?" Brighton asked.

"Uh, no, we just had a feast," Riley laughed. Brighton pointed out the window at a poster advertising a nearby food hall. The poster was admittedly enticing, featuring a collage of classic food porn – burgers, sushi, dumplings, noodles, kebobs.

"I've been meaning to try that place."

"So you wanna go now?"

"Yeah, is that okay?" he asked. "You can just drop me off here if you don't want to come."

"I...well..." Riley looked at the poster. Then at Brighton. He could be a friend...right? People met friends through work all the time. Why couldn't she? Because of those arbitrary rules she made up for herself? Besides, beggars can't be choosers. And in the friends department, Riley was definitely a beggar. So she couldn't be choosy about whose company she accepted, right? "You know what, I'll come with you."

"Okay, great!" Brighton said, smiling a wide smile as he opened the door and pulled Riley out.

18

She sat across from Brighton, a smorgasbord of junk food laid out between them. He had paid for everything, insisting that it was because he was planning on consuming most of it on his own. Riley wondered how some guys could put away the amount of food they did without being three-hundred pounds. Brighton was at that age where guys started to develop those little beer bellies if they hadn't already, and yet there were no signs of that.

In the hustle and bustle of the crowded food hall, conversation wasn't exactly easy. They had to yell a whole lot and lean in over all the greasy foods to hear one another.

But despite the fact that *having* the actual conversation proved difficult, the conversation itself came easy.

Even after all that Riley had since learned, it was surprising to see Brighton engaging in string after string of run-on sentences – sentences that had tangents that lead to new conversations in the midst of the last. It should've been a mess to follow and despite the fact that Brighton's words were like unpredictable, rolling waves, Riley felt like the skilled surfer who knew how to catch every one.

Riley wasn't sure if she was naturally a comfortable conversationalist or if she and Brighton just clicked.

After covering those typical, topical subjects like television, movies, current events, local gossip – Riley could feel a shift into more personal territory. After all, there was no way anyone could talk for an hour about their thoughts, feelings, and opinions without revealing something more about themselves.

At an hour in, Riley was officially no longer on the clock as Brighton's wedding planner. Now they were in each other's company in a completely voluntary manner, ignoring whatever time constraints they previously said they had.

And though Riley had known Brighton for a mere week or so, and this marked only the third time she had seen him, she noted that this was the closest thing she had to an actual friend. Her instinct was to lament over the fact, but it all felt too good to step out of the moment.

The first real pause in conversation was what finally threw her.

Brighton had been in the middle of telling her a story about applying to law school to appease his parents when a young couple strolled by. A baby was strapped to the father's chest while the mother held a little girl's hand, double-tasking as she walked and wiped the melted strawberry ice cream from the toddler's face.

He made no attempt to be subtle, watching them so intently that he had actually caught the father's eye. Riley felt a flush of embarrassment over her new friend's strange behavior, but to her surprise, the father smiled at Brighton. And Brighton quickly returned it before the family disappeared back into the crowd.

"You really like kids, don't you?" Riley asked, breaking the sudden awkward silence. Brighton turned back to her with that same surprised look he always had when returning to the real world. It was a revival of the Brighton that Riley thought she knew. First Impression Brighton. The strange, reserved man that seemed to live just for Sierra. Not the vibrant, fleshed-out Brighton that Riley had come to know since.

"I do, but I don't even know why," Brighton laughed, seemingly embarrassed to confess it. "I think I just had a lot of thoughts growing up about how I would be as a parent. And I'd like a chance to put it into play, you know?"

"Sort of," Riley said, pursing her lips. "But I can't help but think of all the ways I know I'd mess it up. Kind of like how my mom messed me up."

"You don't seem messed up to me."

"I'm just kidding, sort of," Riley replied, realizing she was still talking to a client. It was probably best to hide her neuroses when she was tasked to plan the most important day of their lives. But she also didn't want to build a wall between the openness and comfort she now felt around him.

"So you don't want kids?" he asked.

"I don't know." She wasn't lying. She really didn't know. Evan had convinced her that she didn't. Because *he* didn't. But now that she was on her own, she really wasn't sure. "Did you always know you wanted kids?"

"I think I always thought I'd have them, just because that's what people do," Brighton replied. "But since I met Sierra...I don't know. I guess I would really like to be a father." He removed his glasses, wiping them down with the hem of his shirt. His eyes looked sparkly, even in the dim lighting of the food hall. Riley realized then that he had been crying.

Riley swallowed hard, feeling immediately nervous. She was ill equipped with handling tears, especially if they were coming out a full-grown man.

But Brighton stopped her from having to say anything at all.

"Sierra had a miscarriage," he said. "We found out just yesterday. She just wasn't up for coming in today, but she didn't want to delay the meeting since we're on a time crunch."

"Oh my God, I'm so sorry," Riley said, covering her mouth. Her heart dropped as she remembered how Sierra had said that the whole point of the wedding was to show their future kids those beautiful, idyllic photos of their parents' union. She was pregnant when she had said that. The rush to get married was probably so she wouldn't already be showing on her wedding day.

"No, God. I'm the one who should be sorry," Brighton said, letting out a low chuckle through his tears. He cleared his throat, replacing the glasses on his face and looking somewhat normal again as he stuck a cold fry in his mouth. "We're not paying you enough to be my therapist too."

"Don't be sorry, please," Riley replied. "I'm happy to listen as a friend." The word sounded so awkward on her lips. Brighton had been staring out into space, brows furrowed. But as soon as that word left Riley's mouth, his face relaxed a little. He turned back to her, an appreciative smile on his face.

"Thank you," he said.

"Do you want to maybe head back?" Riley asked. "Maybe we can pack up some food for Sierra?"

"No, she said she wants to be alone. And despite everything in me telling me that I should be with her right now, I have to respect that. So I'm going to hang back for a bit."

Riley frowned. But it wasn't because she felt Brighton was wrong. It was that *she* had gotten their relationship so very wrong. Sierra and Brighton weren't anything like what she and Evan were. It wasn't some secretly toxic, oppressive relationship. Brighton simply knew when to step back, when to give Sierra space.

What it must be like to have a man like him...

She blinked, realizing that she had been wordlessly staring at Brighton, lost in her own thoughts. And to her embarrassment, one of those thoughts was how attractive she found him.

Riley reasoned that she had simply misinterpreted a friend crush as something more. She liked Brighton because they were bonding and she hadn't bonded with anyone in ages. The fact that he was objectively good-looking was just...confusing things.

She looked down, saving herself as best she could in that moment. Her gaze was fixed on the cold fries sitting between them. It was a better option than continuing to stare at Brighton, noting his chiseled jaw and boyish charm.

Brighton's hand crossed her vision, picking up a curly fry and dipping it into some fancy flavored mayonnaise. Then he held it out in front of Riley's face.

"Eat," he said. "I feel rude being the only one eating."

"It's cold," Riley protested, though she was smiling in relief. If Brighton had resolved to move on from that very heavy topic, Riley figured she should follow suit.

"It's even better cold," Brighton replied, dangling the little spring of fried potato. Riley wrinkled her nose in doubt. "Okay, it's not, but it's still kind of crispy."

"Okay, fine!" Riley declared, reaching for the fry. But Brighton pulled it away, swinging it forward just enough to dab her nose with some of the dip. She pulled back, wiping the dip off her nose as she laughed.

"Let's try that again," he said. Brighton reached across the table, presenting Riley with the fry. He raised his eyebrows before lowering his gaze to her lips.

Though she felt strange about it, she opened her mouth, tipping her head back to allow Brighton to feed her the fry. His fingers grazed her bottom lip as he retreated.

Riley blushed. *That felt wrong.* But Brighton didn't seem to think so. He had just gone right back to eating like nothing unusual had happened.

Though she realized now that Brighton wasn't as reserved as she had initially thought, she didn't think he'd be the type to physically feed her. Something about that felt oddly intimate. But then again, if Sierra had tried to feed her the fry, she would've been less taken aback. So maybe it wasn't that weird?

"We're out of napkins," Riley realized as she looked for something to wipe the grease from her mouth. "I'm going to go get some."

She walked over to the nearest booth in the food hall, the place where they had bought the fries in the first place. Next to the cash register was a napkin dispenser.

Riley grabbed a couple before realizing the young female cashier was looking at her. She was smiling in an odd kind of way, as if she shared a secret with Riley. Riley smiled a stiff smile back, one that was meant to be inquisitive, as if to force the cashier to explain herself.

"You and your boyfriend are super cute," the cashier said, twirling a strand of her brown hair.

"Oh, he's not my –"

"Usually I think it's cheesy when couples feed each other, but I can tell you two are like super into each other. Like even before when you guys were buying the food, I just like totally felt your chemistry. I'm so jealous."

"Okay," Riley grimaced. "Thanks."

"Like he still checks you out," the cashier pouted, looking over Riley's shoulder in Brighton's direction. "He was watching you the whole time you were walking over here."

"No he wasn't," Riley scoffed. She looked over her own shoulder to see Brighton's gaze fixed on her.

He looked away as soon as he was caught.

19

Brighton and Sierra wouldn't make it for cake tasting – calling in at the very last minute to cancel. Sierra had made the call herself, apologizing profusely, but not sounding all too bad considering what Riley now knew. Sierra didn't mention the miscarriage, nor did she mention if Brighton had told her that he already told Riley.

The two of them had spent a lot of time occupying Riley's thoughts since that day. Their veneer of perfection had been chipping away and it was all being painted over by their recent tragedy. It was hard to shake the image of Brighton looking longingly at that family in the food hall. The quiet tears that followed.

It was all almost enough to keep her from thinking about the strange way that day ended.

With the canceled appointment, Riley's schedule suddenly opened up to more catch up work on her other open projects. She was kind of looking forward to spending an entire day at the office with Marco, just clearing out checklists and tying up loose ends.

But as luck would have it as of late, she was met with an obstacle as soon as she wrapped her hand around the doorknob to her office.

The door jammed at just four inches open.

It wasn't too unusual. The office door didn't fit quite perfectly in its frame and between the ongoing construction and the wildly changing temperatures of spring in New York, the door would occasionally jam.

She put her shoulder into it, but it only opened another inch.

It was then that she noticed the sea of red inside.

"Riley?" She could hear Marco call from the other side. He sounded a bit frantic. She heard a couple clangs and heavy footsteps before suddenly, the door was opened fully. Riley stepped inside, eyes wide as she surveyed the implausible scene before her.

Marco stood in the midst of dozens of glass and metal vases, spread across every flat surface of her office – all over the floor, on their desks, on the shelves, the windowsills. In the vases were an assortment of flowers. Hundreds and hundreds of flowers. Thousands of dollars worth of flowers. All a bright, threatening red.

"What the hell is this?" Riley asked. Her voice was shrill. She noticed then that Marco had his phone pressed between his ear and shoulder. He held two tall vases in his arms, long stems of red roses brushing against the sides of his face.

"I'm trying to figure it out," Marco replied, surprisingly calm. He was still trying to clear a path for Riley so she could get to her desk. "Maybe there was a mix-up with one of our vendors? I just have no idea how they got in though…"

"These were already all here when you got here?" Riley asked. Marco nodded. How was that even possible? They had been so careful to lock everything up ever since their run in with Evan. "Who are you on the phone with?"

"Building security – they're checking who came in this morning."

"Forget it. I don't need them to tell me," Riley seethed. "Just tell them we need our locks changed. *Immediately.*"

"KIND OF AN EXPENSIVE PRANK, isn't it?" Gabriel said as he set the last vase down on the curb outside. Riley had been reluctant to call him, especially since she had been avoiding him like the plague since she found out his ties to Judy. She had meant it when she said she didn't want to be involved with a man who was so close to her mother, but Riley needed his literal manpower to clear the office as soon as possible if she had any hope to get some work done. "Like what was he even trying to say, do you think?"

"He was trying to disrupt my work day and get into my head. Evan's always loved playing his mind games on me and he's probably just pissed that he can't do it anymore. At least not directly," Riley replied. "But as usual, he's doing it in a way that could look innocuous if I were to report it to the police."

"It's still breaking and entering," Gabriel replied. "You can report that."

"It's useless. There's no proof it was him."

"Security is looking through tapes," Marco said. His arms were crossed as he surveyed the red flowers lining the sidewalk. "And you *should* report it. This is too much."

Oof. Riley frowned. This was the closest Marco had ever gotten to arguing with her. He was definitely as unsettled as she was.

And he was right. She had made it so other people's safety was at stake.

IT WOULD TAKE MORE than cheesecake to make things up to Marco this time.

So when Marco went out for lunch, Riley called his favorite barbecue spot and prepaid for a generous happy hour for him and three friends. It was definitely enough to stuff them silly as well as get them sufficiently wasted. And though it wasn't really something Riley could afford, it felt like a necessary expression of how sorry she was to her poor assistant. He didn't deserve to feel unsafe in his workplace because of her.

When Riley told him what she had done, Marco's eyes went wide with such glee that she wondered why she hadn't done it earlier.

After all, he was deserving of this sort of thing whether or not he had suffered through Evan's terrorizing.

After Marco left, Riley rushed downstairs to Gabriel's studio with a bag full of the same diner food they had ordered the night Riley stuck Gabriel with the bill – black and white milkshake, cheese sticks, and disco fries.

Gabriel's parkour studio was pretty huge, taking up a third of the lower floor. It was recessed below the lobby, which made the ceilings twice as high. Riley walked down the stairs into the studio, marveling at the adult sized jungle gym. To the unadventurous (like Riley, admittedly), it looked like a series of death traps – even with the cushioning of foam bricks and mats below the high bars and rings.

It seemed like class had wrapped up for the day and for a second, Riley wondered if she had missed Gabriel. She would have texted ahead of time, but she had wanted to surprise him. Something about pre-announcing her good deed felt more self-serving than she would've wanted.

Just as she was about to turn and leave, Gabriel stepped out of what she assumed was the locker room. His hair was wet and he had a gym bag slung over his shoulder. When he saw her, his thick eyebrows waggled in a silly manner, as if waving hello.

"I brought you dinner," she called out.

"Dinner! Hell yeah," Gabriel replied, jogging towards her now. "To what do I owe the pleasure?"

"Are you kidding?" Riley wrinkled her nose, laughing. She handed Gabriel the bag. "How about your nonstop help since the day we first met?"

"Sure, I guess." Somehow Gabriel already had a mouthful of mozzarella sticks. Riley had barely caught when he had opened the takeout bag at all. "Sorry, are we sharing?"

"If you don't mind," Riley smiled.

"Cool, then you gotta come home with me because I'm already running late."

20

P enny, Margaret's home attendant, was clearly dressed for
a date.

She was in her late twenties and wrapped in a little black
dress, twirling her blonde blowout anxiously as she peered out the
townhouse window.

"Poor girl," Gabriel said with a laugh. "I told her she could just
leave before I got back if she needed to, but she's far too responsible
to do something like that."

The door was open by the time they reached the front steps.
Penny had her purse slung over her shoulder and was typing mania-
cally on her phone to whomever she was late to see. She was very
much ready to go.

"She's doing great today," Penny said to Gabriel, her attention
still half on her phone. "She's pretty lucid, knew who I was, very
chatty."

"That's what I like to hear," Gabriel said. He and Penny
exchanged quick goodbyes before Penny ran off towards the closest
subway station. Gabriel turned towards Riley. "So it sounds like you
get to *actually* see her today."

"Do you think she'd remember me?" Riley asked.

"Eh, let's not push it," Gabriel said. "If anything, you'll just meet again."

Margaret was standing when they got in, watering the plants that sat on the windowsill. She was wrapped in a wacky looking shawl, as bright and colorful as her hair once was, obviously home-knit with a mix of leftover yarns.

"Mom, you're going to drown those guys," Gabriel said as he locked the door behind him.

"No, it's fine!" Margaret said. Her voice was almost as Riley remembered – energetic, vibrant, full of pure joy. "I touched the soil to check. It was dry." Riley tried to force a smile. It was almost more disturbing to see that she was capable of speaking like this when just the other day she appeared catatonic. It was a wonder Gabriel was dealing so well.

"I brought us a friend." Gabriel alerted Margaret to Riley's presence. As soon as she did, Margaret clasped her hands over her heart.

"Judy!" she exclaimed, rushing over to hug Riley.

"Oh, um," Riley looked up at Gabriel.

"Close enough," he shrugged. Gabriel plopped down on the couch, spreading the diner food over the coffee table.

"It's been so long!" Margaret said, looking at Riley with such deep love and wonder that it actually warmed her.

"Yeah, um, actually I'm Judy's daughter," Riley began, unsure if she should correct Margaret at all. She looked towards Gabriel for cues, but Gabriel was too engrossed in his milkshake to notice.

"No, I know, of course!" Margaret continued. "You're Judy Junior."

"Yes," Riley laughed, a bit relieved. "That I am."

"Jujube," Margaret said. "That's what we used to call you, remember?"

"Not really?" Riley said. She had a faint memory of Margaret nicknaming her Rye Bread at some point. She seemed to really like her food-related nicknames.

"It was a *very* long time ago," Margaret replied. "We called you that because your hair was red like a jujube! And because you were Judy Junior. Judy's baby. Jujube. Isn't it clever?"

"Very," Riley smiled. Margaret beamed at her. But then quickly, her expression darkened.

"We thought we lost you," Margaret lowered her voice, her face serious. She brushed Riley's hair behind her ears, looking at her intently. Riley's stomach flipped, feeling immediately uncomfortable with the sudden shift in the air. She wasn't certain what Margaret was referring to, but she was pretty sure it had to do with the day of her birth. Riley knew Margaret and Teddy saw Judy through her pregnancy when her own father couldn't be there. She didn't know the details, but she knew the trauma of it had deeply affected Judy, enough so that Riley never got the full story.

Riley had heard that dementia could put a person in a different place in time. It seemed Margaret had been sent back to the day of her birth.

"Mom, come eat. Let Riley settle in." Gabriel waved them over. Margaret turned to look at her son before turning back to look at Riley once again. Her expression brightened just a bit.

"Riley," she said. "Dear Riley, look at you now. All grown up."

"Yes," Riley replied, taking Margaret's hands from her face and holding them down at their sides. "I'm totally okay now. Everything is fine."

"Of course, why wouldn't it be?" Margaret asked, her brows furrowed.

"Right, of course," Riley said, not knowing how else to respond. She led Margaret to the couch, sitting her down beside Gabriel.

21

"What do you think?"

Sierra stepped out from behind the curtains, twirling in a strapless lace ensemble with an A-line hem. Her long dark hair floated around her, sweeping across her bare shoulders with a dreamy airiness. It was like time had slowed for Sierra to enjoy this moment.

Riley's jaw dropped, immediately awestruck. If there was ever any question that women that looked like Sierra had the power to make the world move in slow motion, it would be put to rest right in this moment.

Sierra had asked Riley to go dress shopping with her, admitting to Riley what Brighton had already told her – she had no one else to go with her. Riley jumped at the idea, excited to partake in one of those picture perfect wedding moments she had seen on shows like *Say Yes to the Dress*.

Azalea was a small bridal boutique on Atlantic Avenue, specializing in classically cut wedding dresses and accessories. The shop was smaller than Riley's apartment, but was cozily decorated with all the girly touches that Riley could dream of.

Allison, the owner, had greeted them with two flutes of champagne and a dainty plate of white chocolate covered strawberries. After giving Allison a quick rundown on what Sierra wanted in her dream wedding dress, they were presented with a rack of a dozen hand picked pieces to try on.

Sierra looked great in every single one she tried, but it was this simple tea-length gown that brought out her natural beauty and vibrancy.

"I already know this is going to come out wrong," Riley started. Her hands were clasped over her heart. She could feel it fluttering the way it did when Riley was a child watching Disney movies, back when she was still fascinated by princesses. In the presence of the closest thing to a princess she had ever seen, Riley felt like an excited little girl again. "But you look like Vanessa from *The Little Mermaid*. Do you know who I'm talking about?"

"Vanessa is just Ursula in disguise!" Sierra said with mock offense. She slapped Riley playfully on the knee, but it was clear that she was giddy. Sierra turned to look at herself in the mirror. She seemed happy with what she saw. "For real though, I actually couldn't be happier you said that because I always thought Vanessa was so gorgeous and I totally loved her."

"Me too!" Riley exclaimed, laughing. She was already excited by all the champagne and shopping, but she was happy to know that she could potentially bond with Sierra as easily as she had bonded with Brighton. If not, more so, simply because they were both women. "That's why I said it! And you know, *The Little Mermaid* is still my favorite Disney movie, after all these years."

"No way!" Sierra breathed. "Me too!" Her eyes were wide as she turned towards Riley and dropped to her knees dramatically. The hem of the skirt fanned out around her and her hands were clasped over her heart now, mirroring Riley. They giggled like schoolgirls, happily indulging in their mutual silliness.

"Evan used to give me crap for it because he said it was far from the best Disney movie," Riley said, rolling her eyes. "So he used it against me and said I had bad taste."

"He's a boy so he wouldn't even get it."

"I know, right!" Riley said.

"I do sometimes feel silly for liking it as much as I do, though."

"What?" Riley scoffed. "Why?"

"I don't know. I guess because it's a kid's movie."

"Well, we were kids!"

"I know, but...I don't know, I think it resonated with me more than it should have," Sierra laughed. "Like the whole idea of wanting to leave the world you know behind. Because you don't belong. And, you know the whole starting over thing." Sierra looked misty, her eyes far away. Somehow, it made her look even more like a Disney princess. Riley half expected Sierra to be suddenly joined by bluebirds and bunnies, all eager to take Sierra out of her deep thoughts and make her boisterously happy again.

"So, you think this might be the one?" Riley asked.

"Feels like it," Sierra replied, pushing herself to her feet. "I mean, I just had a moment in this dress. I'm Vanessa. So I have to buy it, right?"

"I think so," she nodded. Sierra smiled, reaching out to give Riley a quick pinch on the cheek.

"Thank you for helping me today," she said. "It means so much to me."

"Well, of course," Riley replied. "I wish I had a friend to help me pick my wedding dress back in the day."

"You didn't?" Sierra frowned, looking a bit sad. Riley brushed back her hair, feeling a little embarrassed to have revealed that fact.

"I had Evan, I guess."

"Your own *groom* went dress shopping for you? Isn't that supposed to be bad luck?"

"Clearly it was."

"God, I'm sorry," Sierra furrowed her brows. She put her hands gently on Riley's shoulders. "Listen, I'm so happy we had this experience together. And whenever you're shopping for a wedding dress again, I will totally be there with you."

"That would be nice," Riley smiled. She didn't really believe

Sierra. People said plenty of things when swept up in a moment. "I would have to have some romantic prospects first."

"I'm supposed to believe a pretty girl like you isn't turning men's heads left and right?" Sierra teased. It felt nice to know a woman like Sierra thought Riley was pretty, but it also posed as an awkward reminder that she had perhaps turned someone's head recently. Specifically, Sierra's husband.

But Riley had pushed that image deep down and away. She hoped that both she and that burger cashier had misinterpreted that glance.

Besides, she should be focused on Gabriel.

Gabriel was a gorgeous man that was interested in Riley. After they shared their diner food at his house, he had expressed that he wanted to see her again in contexts outside of their mothers.

But it still felt so strange. Riley remembered introducing Evan to Judy – the whole shebang that came with that. It was one of those dating rites of passages that had to happen and it was weird to think that Gabriel had already known Judy all his life.

"Are you excited to be back on the market?" Sierra asked, dipping behind the curtained dressing room to change.

"You know, I wasn't...but then..." Riley trailed off as she thought about Gabriel. Despite all the complications that would potentially surround a relationship between the two of them, she couldn't help but think of the possibility still.

"Dish," Sierra said, popping her head back out from behind the curtain. "Tell me everything."

"Oh, there's not much to say!" Riley laughed.

"Who is it?"

"Ah..." Riley blushed, covering her face. The last time she had a conversation like this was when she told Mindy about her feelings for Evan.

"Tell me, tell me, tell me!"

"His name is Gabriel."

"Gabriel..." She nodded, considering his name. Then she knitted her eyebrows together. "How do you know him?"

"Ugh, it's so complicated. But essentially, he's my mom's best friend's son."

"Oh, wow, weird," Sierra said, looking like she was taken aback. "Isn't that a bit incestuous?"

"Oh my God, stop!" Riley laughed. "No, I never knew him growing up, he's a little bit older. I just knew his mom."

"Is she happy to know you're dating her son?"

"She doesn't really know..."

"How about your mom?"

"Oh, she can definitely *not* know."

"Why?"

"It's not like she'd disapprove or anything..." Riley began. "In fact, she'd probably be delighted. Like far too delighted. She'd want to get involved to a ridiculous degree. Like plan our dates, tell us when it's time to say 'I love you.' Name our children. She'd just be so overbearing."

"Really?" Sierra stared at Riley. To say she looked surprised was an understatement. "That seems...so...insane."

"You're telling me."

"Well." Sierra tucked back into the dressing area, closing the curtain behind her. She continued to talk as she got changed. "Better that they're involved than not at all, right?"

"It's funny you mention that," Riley said. "Gabriel seemed to think that too. He said his parents were very hands off. When I said that sounded great, he pretty much told me that it was a grass is greener situation."

"I guess you never really know until you're there," Sierra replied. "I had very hands off parents. In fact, they hardly seemed to know I exist."

"Do you still talk to them?" Riley froze after asking the question. She vaguely remembered Brighton saying that Sierra didn't have any family. She had definitely accidentally stumbled into a sensitive space.

Riley listened for Sierra's answer, but there was just silence. In fact, she could no longer even hear the rustling of her clothes as she changed.

"No," Sierra finally said, her voice wistful. She sighed. "They're gone."

"I'm so sorry," Riley replied, squeezing her eyes shut. She really wished she hadn't asked.

"I don't miss them," Sierra declared, stepping back out. She was dressed again in the t-shirt and jeans she had come in. Riley noticed that Sierra was wiping away tears. "So. Um. Subject change. Brighton told me that he told you about the miscarriage."

Riley's eyes went wide. Perhaps Riley was unaccustomed to how new friends talked, but she was surprised by Sierra's willingness to go so quickly from one uncomfortable topic to another.

"I didn't want to mention it..." Riley said. She wasn't sure if Sierra telling her this meant she was *supposed* to acknowledge it. "I just thought we should focus on having a good day today."

"I was really looking forward to being a mom," Sierra continued. "I wanted to do it right. You know, be the parent my parents weren't."

"And you're going to." Riley approached Sierra carefully, reaching a hand out to touch Sierra gently on the arm. "It's going to happen for you guys, I know it."

"I wish I could be as confident about it as you are," Sierra smiled sadly. "But really, I just think I waited too long."

"Don't say that, you're only thirty-five," Riley said, shaking her head. Sierra let out a bitter laugh.

"Only? No. Thirty-five is considered a geriatric pregnancy," Sierra scoffed. "*Geriatric.*"

"Really?" Riley wrinkled her nose. Didn't geriatric mean elderly? "Um. Well, I..." She didn't know what to say. This was one of those topics that made her feel like she was walking through a field of land-mines. "Would you consider...adopting?"

Sierra's brows furrowed.

Shit, wrong thing to ask, Riley thought, immediately regretting continuing at all.

A heavy silence hung between them.

"I want my baby to be my blood," Sierra finally said. "I think adoption is a wonderful thing, but it's not what I had envisioned for myself."

"Blood relatives aren't always all that great," Riley replied. She hadn't meant to extend the discomfort of the topic, but this was something Riley actually felt. So it came out. "When we have kids, we run the risk of them taking on the less favorable aspects of our family. It's a crapshoot. It's clear that we turned out nothing like our parents, but who knows about the next generation? Like our *kids* could turn out like our parents."

"She wouldn't," Sierra blinked, looking almost insulted. "She wouldn't be like my parents, she would be like me. And Brighton."

"Oh, of course," Riley said, shaking her head. Why was she so insistent on making things more awkward? "Of course she'd be like you two."

It was clear now that Sierra had imagined a very specific future for herself, right down to the fact that she'd have a daughter. Riley knew full well that life just never turned out the way you expect it sometimes. It was strange to her that a woman in her mid-thirties had yet to reconcile with that.

To her relief, Allison had returned from the back office. She had previously left them to try on the dresses on their own while she fielded calls and emails. But sensing that they were wrapping up, she had thankfully come to check on them right at that very moment.

As Allison and Sierra discussed the logistics and alterations of the chosen dress, Riley wandered the perimeter of the shop. Allison had decorated the walls with frame after frame of her clients' dresses. They were all posed happily with their bridesmaids, their parents, their grooms.

They were surrounded by picture after picture of happy families.

Riley wondered if they were all as happy as they appeared or if they had just gotten their shit together for that one photo.

"Do you ever think about what your children would be like?"

Riley jumped, startled at the fact that Sierra had sidled up beside her. They were standing in front of a picture of a bride and her flower girl.

"Not really," Riley replied. She thought for awhile, wondering if she should give some canned answer or tell Sierra the truth. Considering how much Sierra had opened up to her, Riley figured it was only fair to tell her the truth. "My mother kind of scared me off giving birth. I know something bad happened when I was born. She had me two months early. She said it was complicated and everything was touch and go for awhile. When she's being particularly overbearing, I remind myself that it was because she thought I was going to die the day I was born. And that it made her a little crazy. But I'm fine now. Healthy. Just, you know, maybe a little shorter than I was supposed to be."

There was a laser focus in Sierra's eyes as they scanned Riley's face. Her attention was wholly on her now. The smallest hint of a tear appeared in the corner of Sierra's eyes and Riley couldn't help but feel bad about *all* the tears she had seen between Sierra and Brighton. It didn't feel right that she had bore witness to so much of their sadness.

Sierra cupped Riley's face in her hands, bending over slightly to look her in the eyes. Riley swallowed, frozen in surprise and confusion. Sierra's mouth dropped open, wanting to speak. But nothing came out. She looked down for a moment, then looked back up to try again.

"I'm so sorry that happened to you," Sierra whispered. "And I'm so sorry to your mother. It must have been so hard for her to feel like she couldn't protect you. She must have felt like it was her fault that this happened."

Riley had heard that many women felt guilty when they had miscarriages, as if they had any control over what happened. But she hadn't expected to upset Sierra to this degree with her own story. Riley was sure that she couldn't feel any more unsettled than she did in this moment, despite all the strange things that had happened to her in the last couple of weeks.

She gulped, pulling her eyes from the intensity of Sierra's stare.

Sierra pulled away, wiping her eyes before pulling her hair up into an efficient looking topknot. Then she turned back towards Riley.

"Okay, so now that we've both saturated this day with all this heavy duty emotional stuff, let's end on a lighter note," Sierra said. Her eyes were mischievous now, and her face had returned almost entirely to normal. As if none of that had happened at all.

"How?" Riley asked, truly wondering if it was possible.

"I want to meet Gabriel," Sierra replied. "Let's double date."

22

Despite the culinary diversity of her city, Riley rarely ever had a chance to try something new. She and Evan never really went out to eat unless they were joining his friends somewhere and salmon sashimi was about as adventurous as she ever got. It was something she had always meant to get better about, especially when some of her clients inquired about more specific catering options. It made sense for Riley to get to know more, not just because of where she lived, but because it would greatly benefit how good she was at her job.

So when Sierra declared that they'd be doing Ethiopian food for their double date, Riley's eyes lit up.

It was exactly the sort of thing that she'd hope Post-Evan Riley would do – casually go on a double date with a glamorous couple, eating foods that the old Riley would call "exotic" but the new Riley would just call dinner.

The excitement was a bit funny to Riley. She knew that people her age in the city she lived in did this sort of thing regularly, but she had only ever been an observer of it all. Evan's friends had always felt like *Evan's friends* and not her own friends. They never treated her like an individual and was never included in group texts or any planning of their nights out. It was as if she was just an extension of Evan. Like she was just a mutant third arm of his or something.

Consequently, Riley actually felt a dopamine rush after something as simple as sending Sierra a selfie of her date night outfit.

Riley had bought a little back dress for the occasion – her first. It was that staple wardrobe piece she read about in magazines for *decades,* but never got a chance to own. She opted for a simple one to start – sleeveless and knee-length with a scooped neckline. Then over that was a slate-colored denim jacket that served as a bridge between the way she used to dress and the way she hoped to dress in the future.

When her phone dinged with Sierra's text back, Riley had expected one of two things – a thumbs up or a thumbs down on her chosen outfit. But she got something a whole lot weirder.

SIERRA: *Love it. Just don't forget underwear ;)*

RILEY'S GIDDINESS over all the girly aspects of date night was quickly replaced with confusion. What did Sierra mean by that?

But as soon as she arrived at the restaurant, her question was answered.

She was first met with a floor to ceiling cubby full of shoes. When the hostess informed Riley of their shoe-off policy, she lamented over the fact that she would have to remove the three-inch boost that her nude stilettos would give her. And only when she was taking them off did she notice the lack of chairs in the dining space.

As Riley plodded barefoot around the seated patrons, she noticed the low wooden dining tables and colorful mats that looked like flat throw pillows. The diners were atop them, sitting cross-legged.

Sierra and Brighton had reserved a corner nook. The carved out little section had dividers made of laser cut sheet metal with intricate designs that scattered the warm light into shapely star patterns onto the walls. An airy, saffron colored canopy hung above a low hanging stain glass lantern.

Four little pillows surrounded the low set circular table and for once, Riley's stature came in handy. She didn't struggle to duck the lantern and maneuver her limbs to fit inside.

Riley sat between Gabriel and Brighton, allowing Sierra the seat closest to the nook's entrance where she could do all the ordering. Though Riley was pretty in love with her chosen outfit, she had kind of wished that Sierra just warned her about the seating so she would have had the chance to opt for pants. Or something like the gorgeous cream-colored jumper that Sierra had on.

But her text back was probably meant to do just that and Riley's lack of fluency in girl talk had her interpreting it literally.

Riley was the only one who had never had Ethiopian food and she was glad that everyone had enough of an opinion on what to order that she could just nod at the descriptions that sounded vaguely familiar. She thumbed through the menu anyway, trying to look as engaged as everyone else did. But just the names of the dishes, everything from *injera* to *wett* looked so foreign to her – well beyond anything she had ever seen before.

But in the company of Gabriel, Sierra, and Brighton, Riley felt exhilarated by all that she didn't know, rather than scared.

A heady, heavy fragrance of butter and spice hung in the air. And as soon as Sierra was done ordering, the server had come around with a bottle of honey wine for the table.

As she sipped from her glass, Riley couldn't help but admire how gorgeous her date looked tonight, despite the fact that his giant frame was forced to sit awkwardly at this tiny table. He was dressed in a fitted black t-shirt over a pair of black sweatpants that somehow looked city chic rather than like gym clothes. And unlike many men who seemed to struggle with sitting cross-legged, he looked perfectly comfortable. Like some bodybuilder yogi.

Though Gabriel had thoroughly appreciated Riley's outfit, his attention was now wholly on Sierra. And she couldn't really blame him. Riley often found it hard to look away from Sierra. But there was something strange about his gaze that Riley couldn't identify. *What... exactly was he thinking?*

She had since learned that Gabriel was a straightforward man. Since that initial omission of truth, he had proved to be the type to speak his mind and simply *be* who he was. There was no façade, no pretense, no attempt to put up walls. At least as far as Riley could tell with her admittedly amateur abilities to read people.

So she should've known she'd get an answer soon enough.

"Sierra, I can't tell if you're confident or just a risk-taker," Gabriel blurted out at the first chance he could. Sierra had just wrapped up some story she had about backpacking through Southeast Asia.

"It's not a risky area to travel in," she shrugged. "Besides, I had Brighton with me."

"No, sorry," Gabriel shook his head. "I was referring to the fact that you're wearing white at an Ethiopian restaurant. Or *any* restaurant, at that."

"Oh!" Sierra laughed. She placed a hand on Brighton's knee, looking over at him as if he had the answer. But as per usual in Sierra's presence, Brighton had nothing but a smile to offer. "First of all, this isn't white. This is *cream*. And to answer your question, I'm just a risk-taker."

"I've seriously been sitting here wondering how *anyone* could be confident enough to eat *anything* in that outfit," Gabriel laughed his booming laugh. Not only did Riley now know why Gabriel had been squinting so intently at Sierra, she suddenly understood why he opted to wear all black. Judging from their first date, he wasn't great at keeping food off his clothes.

When their orders arrived, Riley marveled at the bright and colorful wheels of vegetables and meats arranged atop the *injera*, which she quickly learned was the sourdough flatbread that doubled as a plate *and* utensils. When she realized the full extent of their eating situation, Riley considered the fact that Sierra's risk-taking was a whole other level than she had previously considered.

There was almost zero chance that Gabriel or Riley would make it out of this date without getting tie-dyed by their dinner, despite the fact that they were wearing dark clothes. And especially since the honey wine was being poured with a heavy hand. Despite its syrupy sweetness, Riley could tell that she was about to get very drunk.

Eating proved to be difficult when one was drunk and without utensils, especially when most of the food had the consistency of oatmeal. Riley marveled at how expertly Sierra and Brighton managed to eat. If she were the betting type, she'd put a lot of money on the fact that these two would make it out of the restaurant unscathed. Even Gabriel was doing alright.

Though Riley thought everyone was hungry enough not to notice that she was barely getting any food in her mouth, she should've realized she wouldn't be so lucky. She saw now that Sierra was watching her from the corner of her eye, observing the ineptitude with a subtle curiosity.

"Like this," Sierra instructed, tearing off a piece of *injera* before wrapping it around a bright yellow lentil stew. She held it up, showing Riley what looked like the tiniest burrito, before turning to feed it to Brighton.

In turn, Brighton scooped up some finely chopped beets and put the wrap against his fiancée's lips. Sierra held eye contact with him, smiling as she accepted the food.

The moment seemed a bit too...sensual, or at least intimate, for Riley to be casually observing, but she remembered that Brighton had insisted on feeding her a fry at the food hall and reasoned that this wasn't as weird for them as it was for her. Sierra and Brighton were clearly both the touchy-feely type and this all appeared like perfectly normal behavior to them.

Before Riley could give it a go, she was suddenly presented with a little *injera* wrap herself, held right up to her lips already. She peered over at Gabriel who gave her a quick wink.

"Thanks," Riley said sheepishly, leaning forward to take the bite off of Gabriel. She didn't receive it as neatly as Sierra and Brighton did, and before she knew it, Gabriel was laughing as he swept a thumb over her lips to wipe off the food that didn't make it inside.

Around the time they lost count of the bottles of honey wine they had gone through, Riley's body was dealing with the effects of food coma, inebriation, and a vague but familiar sensation.

A sensation responsible for the fact that she couldn't keep her hands off of Gabriel.

She wasn't sure what sparked this sudden feeling. Perhaps it was all the new and unfamiliar things she had been exposed to tonight. Perhaps it was the wine. All the touching. The sensory overload.

All Riley knew was that she desperately wanted to get Gabriel back to her place. Alone.

But he was still busy socializing, and Riley was admittedly pretty happy just to watch him do that. All the business of feeding each other seemed normal to her now, as if she hadn't been balking at it just a half hour before. She watched as Gabriel moved on to hand-feed both Sierra *and* Brighton and she couldn't help but laugh. They were just strangers an hour before, and now they were acting as if they'd known each other forever.

It all felt sort of out of body, sitting in her new outfit with her new man and her new friends. Doing new things.

Riley marveled at just how quickly things could change.

23

The sunlight that crept through her blinds every morning felt like laser beams today. Riley groaned, covering her already closed eyes with her palms, applying just a bit of pressure to hopefully nudge that dull headache away.

She could feel that she was on the edge of her bed, which was unusual these days considering she slept dead center ever since Evan left. There was also an unusual whiff of something in the air – cologne.

Oh boy, Riley thought. She must've brought Gabriel home after all.

She felt kind of bad that she couldn't remember their first time together, but even worse about the fact that she couldn't even remember how she got home. It had been ages since she drank like that and she definitely *never* blacked out. Riley desperately hoped she hadn't done something embarrassing.

Eyes still closed, she turned towards Gabriel, putting her hands out to feel for him – to confirm he was actually there. Her fingertips met bare skin.

He shifted slightly under her touch, but just as quickly fell asleep again.

His smell was invading her space, amplified for some reason. But there was a touch of something else that struck her. Patchouli. A smell that she didn't associate with Gabriel. A smell she associated with...

Riley's eyes snapped open as she sat up. The sun just about blinded her, but she forced herself to clear her vision, willing her pupils to adjust so she could see for sure who it was lying beside her.

To her horror, it was exactly whom she had thought – Brighton. In nothing but her sheets.

"What the hell!" Riley exclaimed, pushing herself off the bed. She tumbled to the floor before scrambling to get back on her feet. She herself was clothed, but not in the dress she had worn out. Instead, she was in an oversized t-shirt. The one that Gabriel had worn the night before.

She turned towards her bedroom door, only to find Gabriel sprawled out on the ground, snoring peacefully. Shirtless, but pants still on.

Oh my God, what the hell did I do? Where's Sierra?

Riley tumbled out of her bedroom door, in such a panic that she tripped over her own feet twice before regaining her ground. She stood up to find Sierra preparing coffee in the kitchen, peacefully. Still looking neat and unwrinkled in her cream-colored jumper.

"Morning!" she declared, looking chipper. There wasn't a hint of a hangover anywhere on her perfect face.

"What the hell happened?" Riley asked.

"What do you mean?" Sierra looked startled by Riley's distress.

"What happened...like...last night?" Riley felt embarrassed just to say those words, especially with the quizzical manner in which Sierra regarded her.

"Oh...you woke up next to Brighton didn't you?" Sierra laughed. "Aww, sweetheart. That must've freaked you out." Riley blinked at Sierra. That wasn't enough of an answer.

"I don't remember *anything* after ordering dessert," Riley gasped when she realized. "Did...like...what..." She felt like she was on the verge of hyperventilating.

"Okay, okay calm down," Sierra said, suddenly taking her seriously. She poured a cup of coffee from Riley's Chemex and handed it to her. "Everything's fine, nothing happened."

"Why are we all here?"

"You invited us over," Sierra replied. "We agreed since you looked like you needed a little help home anyway. I'm glad we came now since you were apparently a *whole* lot drunker than we realized. Anyway, we got back, ate some leftovers, played a couple rounds of Cards Against Humanity. You passed out soon after so Gabriel carried you to bed."

"Do you know...if..."

"No, you guys were acting like middle schoolers," Sierra laughed. "You didn't do anything. Not even kiss."

"Why was Brighton in my bed...?"

"We all were," Sierra said. "You insisted we didn't leave. And we were all trashed at that point. Gabriel made some joke about us all fitting on the bed if we slept sideways, so we tried it. It worked for some of the night but then Brighton went to sleep on the floor. When I got up before, he got back in."

"Well, he's there alone now since Gabriel is also on the floor."

"I mean, queen sized beds aren't meant for four adults. Especially not when one of them is Gabriel's size."

"God..." Riley said, squinting as she sipped the black coffee Sierra presented her. She felt a whole lot more relieved despite still feeling pretty disturbed. "I haven't been that drunk...ever. I've never actually blacked out before."

"Really?" Sierra looked very surprised. "God, you must've been such a good girl."

"I was," Riley replied. "Like super straight-laced and obedient. It's kind of ridiculous now that I look back on it."

"Well I'm glad you got to live a little last night."

"Too bad it hurts so much the next day," Riley replied. "So what do people do when they're this hungover? Because I will take any and all suggestions to get rid of this feeling."

"Start with coffee, move onto electrolytes."

"Like Gatorade...?"

"Yeah, that sorta thing," Sierra smiled. "God, you're adorable."

"Why, because I got blackout drunk for the first time in my thirties?"

"Yes," she laughed. "But you know, just in general you're just the cutest."

"Thanks," Riley frowned. She hated that word. And apparently she made it clear on her face because Sierra was now frowning too.

"You don't like being called that, do you?"

"No, I'm sorry," Riley said. "In high school, I felt like people were using it in a derogatory way. Like everyone wanted to remind me how small I was all the time. My mother did it too. And Evan. So I've come to hate the word."

"Our past dictates our present," Sierra shrugged. "I get that."

Suddenly, her front door opened.

The chain stopped it from opening completely.

Riley's eyes widened, in shock that this was happening once again. She had had the locks changed, how on earth?

The sharp blades of a bolt cutter suddenly surrounded the taut chain. With a loud snap, the chain was cut and the door was open.

The man who entered was not Evan, as Riley had suspected, but her landlord, Freddie.

They stood staring at each other for a beat, both confused. But then Evan came up behind him.

"What's going on here?" Riley asked. "You can't just break in like this!"

"You can't break into your own home. Freddie was just letting me back into my apartment," Evan replied.

"He didn't tell me you were in here," Freddie said, hands up like he realized something was amiss. "He said he thought someone broke in and locked him out."

"What sense does that make? He doesn't live here anymore!" Riley exclaimed. "I asked you to change the lock to keep him out, don't you remember?"

"His name is still on the lease," Freddie stammered. "In fact, it's the only one on the lease."

"That's right," Evan said. "You never got around to putting your name on there."

Shit, Riley thought. He was right. Her credit had been in the gutter at the time. It was in their best interest to make Evan the sole name on the lease.

"I..." Freddie shook his head. He looked like a man who had messed up, but didn't know exactly *how* he messed up. "I'll leave you to yourselves." Riley listened as his footsteps hurried away from the ensuing drama.

Evan looked over at Sierra, eyes questioning, before returning his gaze to Riley.

"Who is this?" he asked.

"I'm a friend," Sierra answered for Riley.

"Right," Evan sneered, making his skepticism apparent. Riley knew it was meant as a dig towards her, to remind her of her insecurities over her friendlessness. But it didn't really work so well now. Not when she felt confident in calling Sierra a friend.

"What do you mean by that?" Sierra asked, stepping up closer to Evan. Riley tensed. She thought about what Gabriel had asked her the night before – *are you just confident or a risk-taker?* Riley wasn't sure what it was that allowed her to get so close to Evan when Riley was still afraid.

"It doesn't matter what I mean," Evan said. "I don't know you and I don't have to answer to you in my own home."

"This is Riley's home," Sierra replied. "She has as much of a right to it, even if her name isn't on the lease."

"I'm not asking her to leave now, am I?" Evan seethed, getting in Sierra's face. They were almost the same height, almost eye-to-eye. Sierra stood her ground, not the least bit intimidated by him. In fact, in her presence, Evan was beginning to look smaller.

The commotion had woken up the two left in the bedroom. Brighton and Gabriel appeared at the door, both looking a bit disheveled but otherwise intimidating at their size. They were both still shirtless and Riley could now see that Brighton thankfully still had his jeans on under the sheets they were sharing just a little bit ago.

Evan looked bewildered. When he turned back towards Riley, his eyes had switched to accusatory.

"What's this guy doing here again? Who the hell are these people?" Evan yelled. "What are you now? Some kind of slut?"

"Hey!" Gabriel bellowed, marching up to Evan with such an intimidating stance that Evan actually cowered before he could catch himself. "You want me to follow through with what we talked about last time?"

"He's done this before?" Sierra asked. Her eyes were wide with shock and anger. She stepped up into Evan's space some more, making him back into the shoe rack behind him. The expression on Sierra's face was scathing. She stopped only inches away from Evan's face, excelling in the intimidation tactic that Evan had failed at before. "Does it make you feel like more of a man to bully your ex-wife?"

"We're still married," Evan muttered, visibly pissed that he was being threatened by a woman.

"You may have trained her to be scared of you, but you can't fool me," Sierra whispered. "I can see what a sorry excuse for a man you are."

"Back off, bitch," Evan spat. "Before I make you." Brighton stepped forward now, his body tense and ready for a fight. Sierra didn't even have to turn to know what was happening. Instead, she kept her face towards Evan's and held one hand up to indicate to Brighton that he should stop. And he did.

"I'll take that as a threat," Sierra replied, her eyes fixed on Evan's. But she acquiesced, backing off a little and giving him some space. Evan smiled a smug smile, as if that was enough of a win for him.

"Get these people out of my home," Evan said, his voice flat.

"You can't make her leave," Gabriel said. "The law is on her side."

"I'm not asking her to leave," Evan said. "I'm asking *you* to leave.

And these other mystery assholes too. Riley is welcome to stay. We're overdue for a talk, anyway."

"You *left* this space, Evan!" Riley exclaimed. "You can't just invite yourself back in after all that happened."

"You *made* me leave. Illegally. And my lawyer can attest to that," he replied. "And if you don't believe me, you can give him a call yourself."

24

When Riley forced Evan out, he had his options. He had friends who were happy to house him and parents who lived nearby. She hadn't been all too worried about where he'd end up. Wherever it was would be comfortable.

Riley, on the other hand, did not have options, so she found herself suddenly choosing between staying with Gabriel or staying with Brighton and Sierra. Evan had meant it when he said he wanted her to stay, but he had to have been smart enough to understand that there was no way that was going to happen.

Riley grabbed a small go-bag that she had packed at the height of her arguments with Evan, one that she had never unpacked even after he left. It came in handy now when she had to make the speedy exit that she did.

Though neither housing option she had was ideal, Riley settled on staying with Gabriel since he had an actual guest room, something that was considered a luxury in New York City.

In fact, everything about Gabriel's life turned out to be quite a luxury. The fact that he owned an *entire* building put him in a class that few belonged to.

Riley had only really seen the lower floors of his house – just the lobby, the parlor, and the first floor living room. But now that it was going to be her new temporary home, she got the full tour. She learned that Gabriel's dad, Teddy, was an heir to a textiles manufacturer which afforded him the ability to work solely on his art. He was a painter, though he worked with many mediums, and through his community of artists he met Margaret. And though most of the house retained the original, old-fashioned décor that Gabriel's grandparents had chosen for it, Margaret's flairs were seen in odd corners here or there.

And there was no place where it was more apparent than the guest room.

Margaret had a knack for knitting wacky looking items that looked like it belonged on muppets or people marching the Rio carnival, and she had yarn-bombed the guest room in exactly that way. There was the chunky giant knit of the blanket that covered the bed and the finer, wispier knit of a throw that sat on the corner armchair.

Even the curtains were hand-knitted.

Riley was impressed that the house had maintained its specific décor even when so many people had passed through since it was first decorated. She learned that before Gabriel, his oldest brother and his wife and children had lived there before deciding to move to the west coast and that his middle brother had also hung around for a bit before buying a Manhattan penthouse – which was more "his style."

"They're totally the black sheep of the family," Gabriel explained. "My parents thought my nomadic life was much more their stride."

Riley laughed as she unpacked her small bag and set her toiletries on the windowsill. How nice it was that Gabriel got along with his parents, despite his admitted misgivings about their parenting techniques. Riley had never met Teddy, but it seemed like both he and Margaret had raised their children wonderfully, no matter how much Gabriel said they didn't know what they were doing.

Although *maybe* she would get along better with Judy if it meant inheriting a family house. She smirked at her own thought.

"So if my parents moved upstate to be with your parents, do you know why your parents decided to go up there to begin with?" Riley asked.

"They wanted goats," Gabriel replied. Riley paused, waiting for Gabriel to laugh and say it was a joke. But it was pretty clear it wasn't.

"Seriously, that's the only reason?"

"They wanted goats to milk so they could make their own cheese, if I have to get specific."

"God, I wish I knew you growing up," Riley said, a sad smile on her face. "I feel like things would've been different for me."

"We would've had *nothing* to talk about," Gabriel laughed. "The age difference might not feel like anything now, but back then it would've been like the Grand Canyon between us."

"I guess that's true."

"Besides, now we can make up for lost time."

"I wish you had caught me at a better time in my life."

"When would that be?" Gabriel crossed his arms, arching an inquisitive eyebrow. "When you were still with your husband? Five years from now when you'd probably be happily settled into another relationship?"

"I don't know," Riley shrugged. She smiled, knowing the point Gabriel was getting at.

There was never really a perfect time for things to happen.

———

25

T hings turned around quickly.

Living in Carroll Gardens meant a quicker commute to work. Walking with Gabriel meant feeling safe. Knowing that any attempt Evan made now to break into her home (however temporary it was) would result in something they could *actually* call breaking and entering or trespassing.

Riley loved her routine now.

She loved having breakfast with Gabriel and Margaret, saying hello to Penny, going to work with a clear and happy mind. She loved picking Gabriel up from work since she usually wrapped up before he did. She loved how he smelled straight out of the shower, their breezy walks home, having dinner with him and Margaret.

In between all that, she'd grab an occasional coffee with Sierra. And when they weren't doing that, they'd text all day, remarking on everything from clothes they planned on buying to celebrity gossip. Their work relationship was falling by the wayside, feeling secondary to the true friendship that had developed between them. And though they still didn't get a whole lot of non-working face time and only a few weeks had elapsed since they first met, their bond felt deep and genuine. It just further cemented the notion that life could change drastically in an instant.

The only thing that wasn't ideal was that whatever romantic connection she was forging with Gabriel was suddenly suspended.

It was like they had made a silent agreement to avoid progressing anything non-platonic now that they were suddenly roommates. And since Riley had a ton of work to catch up on, she was distracted enough that she didn't feel the immediate need to bring up that discussion.

Especially since she didn't want to disturb whatever incredible equilibrium she was living in now.

Evan had backed off significantly. Maybe all he really wanted was the apartment back. Or maybe all his stalking helped him understand that Gabriel, giant formidable Gabriel, was now always by her side. He wasn't dumb enough to risk another pummeling, right?

But what Riley loved best about the setup was the fact that she had an opportunity to help Gabriel. It wouldn't be nearly as much as he had helped her, but it was something.

Margaret had come to remember Riley, at least on her good days, and they luckily quite enjoyed each other's company. This meant that after relieving Penny from her shift and having dinner altogether, Riley was able to care for Margaret while Gabriel got a chance to breathe.

Gabriel was hesitant at first, as any good son might be. But it was clear that something as simple as allowing him a couple hours to play video games in his room was a necessity he didn't realize he needed.

Margaret was usually a quiet presence. Her bad days were catching up to her and a lot of the times, she would sit in that strange silence again, staring off into nothing. And as hard as it was for Riley to witness that, she felt helpful and useful that she could just be there with her. That she could spare Gabriel of collecting on these awful moments.

She couldn't be happier to finally be something for Gabriel the way he was something for her.

Tonight, Gabriel had a late event at the studio. It was something that was also Riley's doing. A nearby startup had wanted to do a team-building event with their newly hired employees and asked Riley to arrange it. She referred them to Gabriel who was able to finagle a last minute class for them after-hours.

This meant Riley would be with Margaret alone. Completely alone. For the first time since she moved in two weeks before.

To say she was nervous was an understatement. Though Riley knew there was no real difference between Gabriel being home versus Gabriel being a few blocks away at the office, something about this night was giving her pause.

Perhaps it was the idea that she was still worried Evan might try something. That if he was still following her, he'd know that Gabriel wasn't around this time. And if he did decide to break in, that he might terrorize her or assault her when Riley was responsible for the safety of someone else. And not just anyone, but Gabriel's frail, defenseless mother.

And it didn't help that Margaret was having a bad day. The kind that made her sit motionless. The kind that meant she wouldn't be able to run on her own should she have to.

Riley expressed some of these concerns to Gabriel before he left, and he reassured her that they lived in a fortress. He pointed out every security camera in the house and all the various devices that secured every point of entrance. Then he armed the house with the alarm system before reiterating that his phone would be on and the ringer on high.

After the first thirty minutes without him, Riley realized something in the midst of her anxiety.

Here she was again.

Completely reliant on someone else.

Utterly unable to be on her own without issue.

How had the strides she made in her months following Evan's departure been so quickly reversed? Had she made any progress at all if it meant it could be so swiftly revoked?

But her circumstances were unusual though, weren't they?

Stalkers aren't an everyday occurrence and crazy ex-husbands aren't something you do more than once.

Right?

Riley reasoned she wasn't reliant on Gabriel, though. They weren't even dating anymore. They were just friends. She was dependent on him for housing until she figured things out, but that was really it. Their walks to and from work – that was just a nice perk. A normal thing that friends did.

She didn't *need* those things. They were just...there.

Though Riley's room was on the second floor, she brushed her teeth in the bathroom next to the ground floor bedroom where Margaret now stayed. It was easier for her to avoid the stairs and have access to everything she needed.

Riley kept the door open, her ears perked up to listen for Margaret's movements through the sound of her toothbrush. Margaret hadn't eaten yet today. Refused to. Riley hoped that she could get Margaret to put something in her system considering how skinny she had gotten.

As she rinsed out her mouth, Riley made out a change in the ambience.

Before, the only sound that permeated the ground floor was the soft brushing of the yarn that Margaret was winding. She did that sometimes, even in her "bad state" she seemed to like winding and unwinding her yarns.

But now, there was the tiniest hint of a whimper.

Riley wiped her face, rushing to Margaret's bedroom. She half expected to see Margaret had fallen – her greatest fear. That she'd look away for a second and Margaret would do something to hurt herself.

But she was right where Riley left her.

Margaret sat in her armchair by the window, looking out on the street as she continued to wind her yarn. The whimpers continued, making her thin lips shake. Riley approached carefully, peering out the window with her.

There was nothing notable there – just their small front yard and empty, tree-lined street. The branches swayed gently in the night breeze.

"What's wrong?" Riley asked, quietly. Margaret wouldn't turn to her, so she looked at her face through the reflection of the window. There, Margaret's eyes moved to meet hers. Riley could see a clarity that wasn't there before.

"Nothing's wrong dear, why would you ask that?" Her voice was clear again, the same way it was on her good days. Riley smiled, wondering if Margaret had just been struggling to get some words out. Margaret returned her smile.

"Would you like something to eat?" Riley asked.

"No, I'm not hungry," Margaret shook her head. "I just ate." Riley continued to smile, although that wasn't true. Gabriel had said to let Margaret believe what she believed as long as it wasn't hurting her. It was just easier to deal that way.

"I was going to have some dessert," Riley lied. "Maybe you want some? Cookies? Cake?" She had learned that Margaret liked her junk food. Although Gabriel was concerned for her general health, Riley thought it was better to get her to eat anything at all if it came down to that. Margaret's eyes squinted, mischievous.

"Okay," she replied. "Cookies, then. But don't let Little Gabey know, okay?"

"Of course not," Riley laughed

"He's had too much today," Margaret said, pushing herself up from the chair to follow Riley out of the room. "I don't like to dictate what he can and can't eat, but that boy loves his sugar and diabetes runs on his father's side."

"I'll make sure to watch him," Riley joked.

"Thank you for caring for him, Jujube," Margaret replied, suddenly serious. "You are so good to him. That's why he loves you."

"Oh," Riley blushed. She wasn't sure what to do with that information. How Margaret had gleaned such a fact was beyond her. There was rarely a moment that Margaret was alone with Gabriel now that Riley had moved in.

In the kitchen, Riley opened the refrigerator to find the white bakery box of cookies and cake that she had bought for Margaret a couple days before. She took the box out, placing a couple butter cookies and a cupcake on a small plate and presenting it to Margaret.

"How's that?" Riley asked. "Enough?" She smiled a teasing smile. Margaret giggled with delight, taking the plate from Riley before picking up a butter cookie. She bit into it, eyes crinkling with happiness as she savored it for a moment.

"You know, he's always loved you," Margaret said, brushing some crumbs from her lips.

"Did he?" Riley laughed. She felt awkward despite the fact that she liked hearing this.

"He's had a crush on you since he was a kid," she continued. Riley frowned. She remembered Gabriel's instructions to play along, but Margaret had again clearly steered somewhere far away.

"Who did he have a crush on, Margaret?" she asked, hoping she had found a way to get her to clarify without contradicting her.

"You," Margaret replied.

"Who...do you think I am?" Riley asked, carefully. Margaret blinked.

"Jujube," she said with a frown.

"Um..." Riley stared. She figured it was better just to give it up and go along with it again. "I had no idea he felt that way!"

"Oh, for sure," Margaret said, chipper again now that Riley was back on board. "He always liked red hair, you know. But now, all he can talk about is you! He comes home from school and he asks about you right away."

Riley wasn't sure what to say now. Margaret wasn't in the present day, that much was clear. But what was she talking about? Where exactly was she? It wasn't possible that Gabriel had a crush on her when she was a kid. He was almost six years older than her. Hypothetically, if Gabriel had a crush on her at any point in his childhood, it would make him a bit of a freak. Especially because he was seventeen when he last lived at home, which meant Riley was eleven, but looked six.

"What school does Gabriel go to?" Riley asked.

"Purchase. It's just a couple hours from here."

Purchase. It was a state university near their hometown. Margaret was referring to when Gabriel was in college.

"Why does he ask about me when he's home?" Riley continued, feeling the hairs on her neck stand on end.

"He's just curious," Margaret shrugged. "Curious about where you are. He had no idea you were here the whole time!"

"I..." Riley shook her head. She had never met Gabriel as a child, right? He had confirmed that himself. But *had* they met? She was still in middle school when Gabriel started college. She was a junior in high school when he graduated.

"Boy, he would go on and on about you," Margaret laughed. "He would say you were his dream woman. That he wanted to marry you. And he always got along with your mom so he would be happy to be her son-in-law."

"Okay, I get it" Riley said, firmly. Her tone was different enough to throw Margaret off. She felt immediately guilty.

Riley knew that nothing Margaret said really meant anything. She was confusing her timelines, living in multiple decades at once. But Riley would be lying if she said she wasn't thoroughly freaked out.

Gabriel wasn't some pedophile creep, was he? He was into her *now.* Maybe he had mentioned it to Margaret and she just mixed it all up.

Actually, that made sense. That made perfect sense. She didn't know much about dementia, but that was more than likely.

Right?

26

"What're you doing here?" Judy exclaimed as Riley opened the front door.

"Hello to you too, mother," Riley replied.

"Not that I'm not ecstatic to see you, but I'm just surprised," Judy said as she stepped inside. She was holding a bag of groceries in one arm and dragging a suitcase with the other.

Uh oh, Riley thought. A surprise visit. She swallowed hard at the thought of having to live under the same roof as Judy again.

"She lives here now," Margaret said, sneaking up behind them. Judy was so excited to see Margaret in good shape, that she threw her arms around her friend for a tight embrace, ignoring what she had said altogether.

Gabriel widened his eyes at Riley, waiting for Judy to realize.

"I guess my mom called her this time because I didn't," he whispered. "I would've warned you. What are we going to tell her about your situation?"

"I don't know," Riley sighed.

"Let me put my stuff in the guest room and I'll be right back out," Judy said, setting down the groceries and hurrying towards the stairs. She moved much faster than any seventy-one-year-old should.

"Wait, wait!" Riley protested, but Judy had already disappeared up onto the second floor.

As Gabriel carried the groceries into the kitchen, Riley stood helplessly, looking towards the stairs as they waited for it all to dawn on Judy.

Then, Judy came rushing back down.

"Wait, did Margaret say you...live here now?" she asked, narrowing her eyes at Riley.

"Yes..." Riley replied, reluctantly.

"Is that true?"

"Yes."

"Why...?" she raised an eyebrow as she crossed her arms. Immediately, Riley was sent back to her childhood. It had been ages since Judy dared to take this stance with her daughter. Riley heaved a sigh, figuring she should just explain.

"Evan took the apartment back," Riley said. "He kicked me out. Well, not actually. He wanted me to stay, but I couldn't."

"So he wants to get back together?" Judy asked. "Isn't that a good thing?"

"No, because I was the one who ended it," Riley replied. It was a detail she had kept from Judy, knowing full well that an interrogation would follow. It was much easier for her to believe that the split wasn't Riley's decision. There was just too much to explain.

To her surprise, her mother decided to spare her.

"So I guess we'll be roommates this weekend?" Judy asked, clapping her hands together.

"I'll sleep on the couch," Riley replied.

JUDY AND MARGARET chattered happily over their *mise en place* as they continued to prep the ingredients for the chicken pot pie they had planned to make for dinner. Riley was thankful her mother had reverted to the minimal-questions mode she had taken on in the last ten years, opting for the occasional judgmental glance in lieu of an onslaught of personal interrogations.

She sat on the couch, flipping through her phone looking for some sort of city event happening this weekend, just so she could have an excuse to get out of the house and away from her mom. Riley wondered if Sierra would be free to join her.

Gabriel quickly caught onto what she was doing.

"It's rude if you leave," he said, quietly. "Your mom's really excited about us eating together."

"I can only take so much of that woman at a time," Riley whispered. "It's only a matter of time before she's pressing me on what's going on with Evan and I'll be forced to tell her that he's gotten violent and there's no chance of things getting better and then she'll freak the hell out and try to micromanage my life again."

"You have to give her some credit," Gabriel said. "She's already pretty restrained, considering."

"That's because she doesn't know what you know," Riley huffed. "And I'd like to keep it that way."

She thought again about what Margaret had said the other night when Gabriel was out. Riley had wanted to mention that to him, but she couldn't figure out a way to ask it without sounding like a paranoid freak. In the moments before she fell asleep, she wondered if Gabriel had for some reason secretly stalked her when she was in high school.

"Are you sure we never met in high school?" Riley blurted out. Gabriel didn't detect the accusatory tone in her voice.

"We weren't in high school at the same time," Gabriel replied.

"I mean when *I* was in high school," she said. Her voice was a bit aggressive, she could hear that. She was feeling a little less inclined to protect Gabriel's feelings now that he was siding with her mother.

"Not that I can remember," Gabriel said, his brows furrowed. He looked like he was actually trying to recall. Maybe he was just a good actor. Maybe he had planned how to react to all these incidents. Only then did the question strike him as odd. He looked at Riley with a quizzical expression. "What's going on?"

"Your mom said that you would come home from college asking about me," Riley said. "But I was pretty sure we had never met."

"I don't think I did that," Gabriel frowned. "Maybe I asked how Judy was because I knew your mom and knew that she was my mom's best friend. But I would just be making conversation."

"She said you had a crush on me back then," Riley continued. "That you were always into red hair."

"I didn't *know* you back then," Gabriel replied. "And wouldn't you have been like twelve or something?"

"Something like that," Riley said, flatly.

"So what are you talking about?" He looked genuinely confused. It was almost kind of sad to see this hulk of a man with a perplexed puppy dog face.

"I don't know anymore."

"Don't let the things my mom says get to you," he said. "She's said some...weird things since all this started. Everyone says it's pretty typical of dementia. She might've grabbed stuff from headlines or television. She doesn't know what's real anymore, and therefore, neither do we."

"But so far anytime she's done something like that, we've figured out that she's just jumped back into a different time of her life, right? So I just thought she was referring to something I didn't know about..."

"She definitely mixes up what happened when," Gabriel agreed. "But I *definitely* didn't have a crush on you then because I didn't know you *and* you were a child."

"That's what I thought..."

"But..." Gabriel raised his eyebrows. "I did maybe mention to her that I have a crush on you *now*." He smiled at her, brushing her hair behind her ears. "And I really, *really do* like red hair."

"My hair is auburn."

"I like all shades of red," Gabriel replied. "Even the shades your face is turning now." Riley pressed the back of her hand to her warm cheeks. Gabriel laughed, cupping her jaw in his hand. She smiled, though she didn't want to. She wanted to continue with her skepticism, to be on high alert. But she was realizing more and more that with Gabriel, there wasn't really anything to be suspicious of.

27

J udy and Margaret baked the pies in individual servings. They used small, oval-shaped ramekins, blanketing the filling with a buttery homemade crust that had a heart-shaped cutout in the middle.

It was exactly how Judy used to make it for Riley and it was one of the best memories she had of her mother. She felt a tinge of pain in her heart.

Maybe Gabriel was right that she had been too rough on her mother. Riley was sure Gabriel wished that his mom had the ability to carry about as Judy was able to. Perhaps she was taking their time together for granted.

But it was a bit different with her and Judy. Gabriel grew up with two parents and two siblings. Whether the love and attention Margaret paid to him was good or bad, it was equally divvied up among the others.

Judy's concentrated love and attention was suffocating to Riley. It was just the two of them, always. They were both pretty much friend-less hermits that only ever had the other one to look at. It was definitely Judy's fault for not branching out beyond Margaret or finding work that took up more of her brain space. All her energy was so Riley-focused – so determined to make her happy and perfect that it only served to do the opposite.

No matter what Judy's intentions were, it had thoroughly messed Riley up. And even into adulthood, Riley felt an intense pressure just being around her.

But now, in this setting, it was kind of nice.

Judy's attention was split among everyone, evenly. Perhaps a little more attention was paid to Margaret, knowing how brief her moments of clarity could be. As they sat around the dining table, the four of them felt like a family. Two adults. Two "children." This was the setup that Riley had always craved. The nuclear family. Their fathers weren't there, but that feeling of wholeness was present.

She always wondered why Judy never dated again. She had said that her father was the love of her life, that there was no one else in the world meant for her after she lost him. But she had lost him so early. She was only forty. Nowadays, in New York, it wasn't even unusual that women were still single and never married at forty. And yet, back then, Judy had just...given up.

It's not like Riley didn't feel sympathy for her mother. It's just that she had limitations with how understanding she could be, especially when her own life was at stake.

But now, without Evan, on the cusp of a new life, maybe it was time for Riley to reevaluate her relationship with her mother. Maybe it was a step she was supposed to take at this juncture.

"So, um...Mom," Riley began. Everyone looked up, as if they were all so surprised that she was voluntarily starting a conversation with Judy. The hopefulness in Judy's eyes made Riley nauseous. "Gabriel said that you guys moved upstate to be closer to Margaret."

"That's right," Judy said with a stiff smile. She definitely wasn't used to talking to Riley about this topic.

"We're very close," Margaret said with a nod. "It was hard to be so far apart after years of living so close together. And Robert and Teddy had gotten close too, so it just made sense that we were all nearby.

And even more so when we had children. So we could care for each other. It takes a village, you know."

"Right..." Judy trailed off. Riley could tell this wasn't a topic she wanted to discuss. But she just wasn't sure why. Maybe the mention of her father. Judy never liked talking about her husband beyond referring to him as some ever-present angel. Stories about him in life were limited. The same ones were repeated over and over again.

"I taught your father how to braid your hair," Margaret said, looking square at Riley. "Fishtails. Judy didn't know how to do fishtails and you liked those. But you were too young to do them yourself." Riley frowned, shooting an apologetic look towards Judy. She knew she had gotten Margaret started on a dangerously sensitive topic. Hearing confused, made-up stories about Robert was exactly what would send Judy into one of her tizzies. And she was long overdue.

"Margaret," Judy said gently, putting a hand over hers. "Robert never met Riley."

Margaret stared into space for a moment.

In the tense silence, Riley hung her head. Her feeble attempt at bonding with her mother had gone horribly awry. Why couldn't they talk about...something innocent? Like flowers or knitting? Or work, even? What on earth was Riley thinking with this topic? She had so quickly ruined what would've been a lovely evening for her and Gabriel and their mothers.

"Yes," Margaret blinked. "I know that. How sad that you never met him. He would've loved you."

"Of course he would've," Judy said, shaking her head. She shot Riley a sad look, as if *she* was the one sorry for all this. Judy kept a firm hand on Margaret's. Perhaps too firm. Riley could see Margaret's crepey skin reddening under Judy's touch.

"Mom," she said, glancing down at Margaret's hand to alert her.

"Oh!" Judy said, retreating as if she had touched a hot stove. Margaret didn't seem to notice. Neither did Gabriel.

"This..." Gabriel cleared his throat. He had been the only one eating this whole time. "This pie is as good as I remembered. Remind me – which one of you came up with the recipe?"

Margaret and Judy immediately dissolved into giggles. There must have been some sort of inside joke here. Why was Gabriel such a natural at this? Why did he know how to talk to them when Riley was so bad at it?

"It was a team effort!" Margaret declared.

"No!" Judy argued. "It was *my* recipe."

"But I improved it!" The two women tittered, grasping each other's hands happily. It was like peace had been instantly restored.

Gabriel reached a hand underneath the table to take Riley's. He gave her a comforting little squeeze, as if to acknowledge her attempt. Even though it failed. Riley sighed, feeling just a bit relieved.

The doorbell rang, interrupting Judy and Margaret's schoolgirl giggles.

"Who's that?" Judy asked. "Are you expecting someone?"

Gabriel shot Riley a quick glance, as if to tell her to keep still and stay quiet. They had discussed their plan of action should Evan decide to find her there. Gabriel would answer the door, Riley would stay close to Margaret and call 911.

But the moment Gabriel opened the door, Riley knew it wasn't Evan. She could hear the crackle of police radios, the stiff sound of shifting canvas, the heavy clomps of thick rubber soles.

"Is Riley Fisher-Wolf here?" a gruff male voice asked. Riley's heart stopped at the sound of her full name. At the fact that she knew something was very, *very* wrong. She rushed to the door, ignoring Judy and Margaret's concerned questioning to find herself looking at two uniformed policemen, one thin, one husky.

"I'm Riley," she said.

"And your husband is Evan Wolf?" the husky policeman asked.

"Yes..."

"Mrs. Wolf," he greeted. "I'm Officer Mayweather. May we come inside?" Riley looked up at Gabriel. He nodded.

Gabriel closed the door behind the policemen as they stood

awkwardly in the foyer. Judy and Margaret were huddled nearby now.

Officer Mayweather drew in a deep breath.

"Everyone's family?" he asked, indicating the group.

"Yes."

"Mrs. Wolf," he repeated, looking at her with a stern expression. "We believe your husband was involved in an altercation earlier this evening. Ma'am, I'm sorry to inform you that he has died."

28

Officer Mayweather had informed Riley that Evan had been out drinking at a bar in Crown Heights when he had gotten into an argument with someone there. The bartender claimed it was over something petty – sports maybe. He wasn't sure. Surveillance footage showed that Evan was later jumped a couple blocks outside the bar, by two men they suspected were the people Evan had gotten into the disagreement with. There was what appeared to be a bit of a fist fight before Evan was knocked down, hitting his head hard on the concrete pavement.

The two men escaped and were still at large.

At Evan's funeral, everyone talked about how uncharacteristic it was for Evan to be physical, let alone violent. They acted as if he was purely a victim in this. And though he was the one who lost his life, Riley knew an Evan that no one else did. Riley knew he was definitely the instigator.

But Riley couldn't say that.

Not now. Not ever.

Now, she was forced to be the mourning widow. A widow who secretly couldn't feel as sad as she thought she should under the circumstances.

She had tried to force out some tears in the presence of his friends and family, just to look normal, but all she could muster were tears of anger.

She was angry at Evan for putting her in this position but angry *for* him and for those who loved him as well. She was angry that he had to die in such a senseless way. But most of all, she was angry that he had managed in death to put her in yet another awful situation.

He died with their names still bound together.

He made her his widow when she only ever wanted to be a divorcee.

MOVING BACK into her apartment didn't feel as morbid as she had expected. Everything was just about the same as she had left it before Evan had driven her out.

His parents had come in to help her pack up his things and Riley had the pleasure of awkwardly navigating a conversation that revealed they had never learned the full details of her separation from his son. They were worried for how she was handling his death, not knowing that Riley had moved on from a life with Evan well before all this happened.

It took weeks to fend off all the condolences, mostly through email since none of Evan's friends had her new number. If they called or texted, she wouldn't know. The last email she opened was from a mere acquaintance of Evan's – the girlfriend of an old college friend who thrived on spreading gossip. She had decided to dutifully "inform" Riley that Evan's family somehow blamed her for his death. Considering how he likely portrayed their split to his parents, they had come to the conclusion that his devastation drove him to drink, which drove him to his aggressors, which drove him to his death.

Riley shut the email, knowing that was the last one about Evan that she would open.

After cleaning the apartment of Evan's half of the stuff and coming across a *very* old expired box of condoms, Riley realized something.

She hadn't taken her birth control in some time. In the insanity that had been her life these past few weeks, she hadn't bothered, especially since she was no longer sexually active.

In the stress of it all, she hadn't kept track of anything regarding her personal health and it was only when she sat down on her bed and opened her non-work calendar that she realized her period was two weeks late.

She knew this was typical of women dealing with stress and that combined with the fact that she had inadvertently stopped her pills meant that her period was about to be out of whack. Riley figured she should just start up the pills again for consistency's sake, but realized that she hadn't even seen them in some time.

For now, it was better that it was delayed. Her period was just another force to be reckoned with among the crap load of things that had piled up for her to handle.

Though event planning was Riley's forte, she had never planned a funeral and planning a funeral had been *draining*. Not just emotionally, but physically. There was so much involved, so many people to inform. And considering the traumatic, unexpected nature of Evan's death, it was all the more difficult to let people know.

And putting her life on hold for that week meant a backlog of work that she needed to deal with as soon as she got back to the office. There was no real time for stress relief of any sort and now that she was living alone again, she lacked the comfort of knowing she'd return home to Gabriel and Margaret – something she had gotten used to.

Gabriel had insisted she continued to stay with them, but Riley thought it was best to spare them of the mess she was now. They had already done so much for her and she wasn't about to add to their existing burdens.

Besides, she was embarrassed by the fact that she brought them nothing but stress and mayhem. And because she was already so stressed on her own, she didn't need the *additional* stress of waiting for yet *another* awful thing to happen. And she definitely didn't want Gabriel to witness any more of it.

Riley hoped he'd understand the distance she needed now. She hoped there'd still be a chance for them when she was ready to rejoin the world.

SIMPLY THINKING of her period had apparently summoned it.

Somewhere in the middle of preparing her dinner of boxed mac and cheese, Riley could feel those familiar cramps. She was down to one tampon and it was just one of many household items that she hadn't restocked since her life went to shit.

There was something comforting in the mundane nature of deciding on what size box of tampons she wanted. Riley had narrowed her choices to the 18 and the 36 pack. She picked up both boxes, weighing them between her hands as if she were a scale, not worried about looking silly in the near-empty pharmacy she stood in.

Riley reveled in the simple task, allowing herself to pretend that this was just another normal day. She thought about all these simple, eventless days that awaited her in the future – perhaps a year from now – where she would have the pleasure of running errands with nothing to worry about, nothing to fear. She'd remind herself then how lucky she was that life had settled into a routine again. She'd recall how awful these days were and note how lucky she was to come out of it alive. There would never again be a day where Riley would mope about being bored or be upset over the humdrum routine she had fallen into. She knew now how great a humdrum routine could be.

She let her eyes wander around the twenty-four hour Duane Reade, wondering if there was anything else she needed. She loved shopping when no one else was around, as if the quietness helped her remember all the things she needed to buy on that list she never bothered to put together. Toothpaste maybe. Toilet paper? Paper towels?

But as she did, she caught sight of the surveillance camera's image of her in a mounted television a couple aisles down. From the overhead shot, Riley looked more tired than ever. The bags under her eyes were so pronounced that she could make them out even from a distance.

And it was then that she realized that she wasn't the only one shopping in the Duane Reade. There was a person on the other side of the shelf where she stood now.

Even under the fluorescent glow of the drug store, the person remained a dark, looming figure – as if it absorbed all light. It reminded her of the shadow across the street. The threatening silhouette that had followed her home after her first date with Gabriel. The way Evan looked that day in her office.

Riley held her breath.

She hadn't even heard any sounds coming from the other aisle. She was sure she was the only one shopping. Could this be some sort of...optical illusion? The figure didn't move. Just stood there like Riley's shadow.

With the boxes of tampons in hand, Riley inched over to the end of the shelf, determined to catch a better glimpse of this figure. For all she knew, the camera had caught something that wasn't even there. Perhaps a fly that was sitting on the lens or something.

She kept an eye on the surveillance camera as she moved just out of frame.

Riley took a deep breath, rounding the end cap so that she could look down the aisle where the figure stood.

Just as she did, the figure turned away from her.

Oh my God, he's actually there, Riley thought, her heart stopping.

She could see clearly it was a man now, tall, dressed in a black trench coat and a black hat and scarf like some sort of cartoon spy. He was racing away from her now, making a beeline for the front door.

"Hey!" she yelled. Riley dropped the boxes of tampons, running into the streets and after the man. *He was real. He's there. He was following me. There's no question.*

But who was he? And why was he following her?

Evan was dead.

So it wasn't Evan.

Evan was dead.

So any person he hired would be off his payroll.

Evan was dead. Evan was dead. Evan was dead.

Which meant that whoever this guy was had nothing to do with him.

29

S he lost him not even two blocks from the drug store.

Riley wasn't sure what she would've done even if she had caught up with him.

She made her way back to Duane Reade when she felt confident that the man had gone far enough off in the opposite direction of her building.

Back in her apartment, Riley restocked her bathroom cupboard with the 36 count of tampons she had returned to buy. There was at least enough for another few months. But the apartment's lease expired in two. And without Evan's name on it, Riley would have to apply again on her own if she wanted to stay.

Or she'd have to figure out what to do next. Where she'd go.

Because clearly, where she lived was compromised.

Riley shut off all the lights in her apartment, standing in the dark as she decided to work off a hunch.

The man in the drug store was the man that had been following her this whole time. The man in the drug store was the shadow. The man in the drug store was the looming, hunched over figure in the empty construction site across the street.

He was *definitely* following her. She wasn't crazy. He wasn't Evan like she had thought. But she knew of his existence now. She could follow him right back. She could get down to the bottom of this once and for all.

Riley crept over to the window, her iPhone open to the video recording function. She knew he would eventually make his way back there, stationed in the window across from hers, watching her every move.

And she was going to find out who he was.

She crouched, peering out the crack at the window where she had once seen him and the flash of what she knew now to be his camera.

She waited.

And waited.

But there was nothing. Not even after her eyes had adjusted to the dark did she see any hint of someone there.

Of course not, Riley thought. She had almost caught him earlier. Why would he put himself in yet another compromising situation? No spy was so stupid to make that mistake twice in one night.

But what if I go out? Maybe that would trigger something. If someone was following her, they would want to know where she was going.

Maybe she just needed to be a lure.

RILEY CHOSE a nice cocktail bar in Cobble Hill.

If she was going to go out alone on this mission, she might as well enjoy herself.

It was 10pm on a Thursday and the dark, wooden space was peppered with couples whispering over fancy drinks, picking at the bar food that sat between them.

The hostess led her to an empty table, mercifully next to another table that only hosted one, single person instead of the couples that swarmed the place.

To her surprise, it was someone she knew.

"Brighton?" Riley said, squinting at the hunched over figure by the fireplace. He had gotten prime real estate for someone without a date.

Brighton looked up. He was wearing his thick-framed glasses, dressed in his uniform of a plaid shirt and jeans. He seemed shocked to see her.

"Riley, oh my God," he breathed. He stood up, scooping her body into his arms and hugging her so tight that her feet almost left the ground. "I'm so sorry about Evan. I'm sorry we didn't make it the funeral. I know you guys weren't together anymore, but what a horrible thing for you to go through."

It was horrible, alright. But it now felt like just one of *many* horrible things. Her life managed to make something as traumatic as her husband's sudden death seem like the least pressing issue.

"Thank you for the flowers," Riley said. "I meant to text, but things have been...hectic." He and Sierra and sent her a beautiful bouquet of pink peonies after they learned about Evan. It felt strange that everyone was suddenly helping her mourn a man who spent the last weeks of his life posing a constant threat to Riley's safety and security.

"Do you want to join me?" he asked.

"Um, sure," Riley replied. She took the seat across from him, feeling the warmth of the fireplace making its way to her exposed shins. She looked around the room, looking for anyone new who had entered who resembled her stalker. But no one new had come in at all. "Where's Sierra tonight?"

"I don't know," Brighton sighed. Riley could smell now the alcohol on his breath and clothes. This cocktail was definitely not his first.

Uh oh, Riley frowned.

"Is everything okay?" she asked.

"I don't know," Brighton repeated, removing his glasses and wiping them with his shirt. His voice was flat. It didn't invite her to further inquire.

Even so, she wanted to ask him what was going on, but Riley was still distracted by the initial goal of her night. The whole point of being out was the hope of luring the dark figure out of the shadows. But she hadn't felt anyone following her on the way to the bar. And she didn't see anyone sketchy sitting around her. Perhaps she should've asked to be seated closer to the window...? Or maybe that person was already out there now? Waiting for her?

Was it better that she had run into someone she knew? Safer, probably. But would Brighton's presence scare him off?

Brighton drank from his glass, bending the swizzle stick over the edge of the lowball. After his initial surprise over seeing Riley, Brighton had receded into a surly disposition – nothing she had ever seen on him before.

"Do you want to talk about it?" she prodded, albeit reluctantly.

"I don't know if that's appropriate," Brighton said. Riley blushed immediately. She wasn't sure why his statement had made her feel so embarrassed.

"Oh, it's fine we can talk about something else."

"I only say that because, you know, you're our wedding planner," Brighton continued. "And I feel like...I don't want you to think that we're not necessarily going through with the wedding based off the things I might say."

"Oh," Riley said. That made sense. Though now she was extra concerned. "Is that a possibility? That the wedding's not happening? What's going on?"

Brighton bit back his lower lip, looking away as he thought. He pressed his knuckles to his mouth and it was then that Riley noticed a long cut on the cupid's bow of his upper lip.

She squinted at him through the dim lighting. There was the tiniest hint of a green splotch under his left eye. A bruise. A black eye that was struggling to heal.

Riley thought about how Sierra had gotten in Evan's face, how intimidating she was in that moment. She thought about how Evan cowered. How even he had instinctively known to fear her.

Then she thought about what that might mean for Brighton. As much as Riley had come to love Sierra and as much as Brighton seemed to love her too, there was no denying that he was a different person in her presence. He seemed suppressed and scared, obedient in a way that no longer appeared healthy.

She wondered about how she had initially suspected Brighton was to Riley as Sierra was to Evan. She considered the fact that she had thought Evan to be incapable of violence, only to be proven wrong.

Had Sierra hurt Brighton? Was he in the midst of his own awakening?

Riley and Sierra hadn't texted much in the weeks following Evan's death. There was just too much going on to talk like normal. And as close as she felt she had gotten with Sierra, she knew now that it'd be naïve to think she knew her.

But could she really be capable of hurting Brighton?

"I promise I won't judge," Riley finally said. "Say what you need to say. I won't let it get in the way of my relationship with Sierra. But if you need to talk, if you need help...you need to say something."

Brighton looked back at Riley, lowering his hands back to the table. Riley noticed the scratches and scrapes across his fingers. Had they been there before? She was pretty sure they had. He was a wood-worker so it would make sense...but in light of the black eye and busted lip, it felt nefarious.

"After eight years together..." He struggled to maintain eye contact with Riley. "I still don't really know her sometimes. I can't predict her. And I'm starting to realize that maybe...maybe I'm afraid of her." Brighton didn't need to tell Riley that. She had sensed it early in knowing them. But then she had thought she was wrong. After all, they were more often good than not.

"I felt that way about Evan," Riley said, sympathetically.

"I could tell," Brighton said. A sad smile broke across his face. "For the most part, I know how to read her now. But when I'm wrong, I'm on edge for days. I'll do anything for Sierra. I love her. I love her more than anyone I've ever loved. I'll do whatever she asks as long as she asks. But sometimes she doesn't *ask*. And I'm left to guess. And it feels like this dangerous game I no longer know how to play."

A pretty blonde waitress had swooped over, dressed in a tight black cocktail dress with her little notepad ready to take Riley's order. She had interrupted at the worst possible time, but she didn't seem to notice.

Riley flipped through the menu as if she had already chosen something, though she knew full well she hadn't the slightest clue what to order. Eventually, she settled on a Dark and Stormy and watched as the waitress strutted away.

Their fight to look normal in front of the waitress seemed to have residual effects. When their attention returned to each other, it was as if they weren't talking about anything bad at all.

"Do you want to talk about something else?" Brighton asked, seemingly eager to capitalize on this inertia.

"If you want," Riley replied. But she didn't want him to move on. She wanted to hear more. She would feel terrible if she learned later that she had been so blinded by the prospect of Sierra's friendship and the business of their wedding at the expense of Brighton's life. But she couldn't bring herself to say those things. It sounded awfully melodramatic.

"I feel like I need to balance out the bad things I said about Sierra really quickly," Brighton said, clearing his throat. "I really love her. We just got into a small fight earlier today and she ran off and I was on my own and...sometimes I feel like without her, I don't know who I am. And because she was ignoring me, it just made me start to wonder, you know?"

Oh boy, did Riley know.

She had had the same thoughts with Evan. She had very much been there. If this is how Brighton had been feeling, then there was no doubt that Sierra was mistreating him. She just knew this with what she'd observed of them. From what she'd experienced on her own. And Sierra and Brighton had been together eight years – just about the time into Riley's relationship with Evan where she realized something wasn't quite right.

But not everyone's experiences were exactly the same. There was no reason to believe that Sierra's treatment of Brighton would escalate into what happened with her and Evan. It was possible that they were just hitting a little rough patch. It was normal for people to have these thoughts before committing to each other forever.

What wasn't normal was the busted lip and black eye.

"I have to ask what happened," she blurted out.

"Huh?"

"Your eye. Your lip. What happened?"

"Oh..." Brighton ran a thumb over his lip, thoughtfully. Riley tried to interpret his expressions, read his thoughts. She couldn't outright ask if Sierra had done that to him, but she had to know. "I had a little accident at the studio."

"What exactly?"

"Uh..." He closed his eyes tight, scrambling for an answer. "Ran into a beam."

It couldn't have been more unconvincing. Brighton was not a skilled liar.

"And it got your eye too?" she asked, knowing she sounded like she was prying now. She could see it on Brighton's face, surprised that she was pushing for so many answers.

"Yeah," he said.

The waitress returned with Riley's drink. She wrapped her fingers around the glass, feeling the condensation build up again her skin. Riley stayed frozen there, not sure where to take the conversation next. Not when she had made it clear what she was implying.

"This was my own fault," Brighton finally said. "I know what you're thinking."

"Only because I'm genuinely worried," Riley replied. Her voice cracked, and it was then that she realized she was crying. The stress of everything had compounded, breaking her in that moment.

"No, stop, don't be," he said, reaching across the table to pry her hand off her drink. He intertwined his fingers with hers until they were palm to palm. "Everything is fine. I know Evan has really thrown things off for you and I really appreciate you looking out for me. But I promise you it's not like that. Okay?"

"Okay," she nodded. Riley wasn't sure if she should believe him, but for the sake of her sanity, she chose to.

"It's nothing like what you're thinking," Brighton continued. "Things are going to go as planned, the wedding is still going to happen, everything will smooth out soon."

"I hate that I'm making you comfort me," Riley laughed through her tears. "I feel so emotionally sloppy. Like I'm running around begging for consolation all the time. No wonder everyone sees me as tiny and defenseless. I don't want to be like this anymore."

"You've been through more these past few weeks than most people go through in a lifetime," Brighton said. "I think you're allowed to look for consolation outside of yourself. And I'm happy to provide it." Riley peered up at him through her lashes, touched by his genuine kindness. She thought about how she had bonded with him first, before Sierra. How they were able to talk in that free-flowing manner that she loved.

She thought about telling him everything. About what she suspected. About the man that was following her.

But she didn't want him to think she was crazy.

So she changed the subject.

"Did you guys cross some things off the wedding checklist while I've been missing in action?" Riley asked. "I'll be back on task as soon as I get back to the office next week, I promise."

"We're still refining the guest list," Brighton replied. "And I think Sierra said she got the dress altered a little but that it didn't take much since she pretty much fit it off the rack."

"I was there when she tried it on," Riley said. "It didn't look like she'd need alterations at all." She thought about the princess that Sierra appeared to be that day. Riley wondered if it was possible that she could be capable of violence.

"What's the dress look like?"

"Oh, I can't share that without her permission."

"Why not?"

"Isn't it bad luck or something?"

"Only if I see it. Not if I know what it looks like."

"Ugh, fine," Riley laughed. She knew Sierra probably didn't want her to share the details with Brighton, but this seemed like the pick-me-up that Brighton needed. A little secret between Riley and Brighton to bond them, but one that would liken Brighton's thoughts of Sierra to something more positive – their upcoming wedding.

"Tell me." A mischievous smile crept across his face. His handsome, boy-next-door features looked different in the dark lighting, especially now that it had been a bit roughed up. Riley took a quick sip of her cocktail, furrowing her brows over her observation.

"Okay. So. It's a strapless gown with a structured sweetheart neckline. And it's tea-length, A-line skirt. It's simple but gorgeous," Riley said, imagining the beautiful dress again. Brighton's eyebrows were raised, like he was happy to know now, but was still somehow confused. "None of those words meant anything to you just now, did it?"

"Yeah I have no idea what that means," Brighton replied, laughing. He seemed to perk up now, sitting up a bit in his chair as he drank from his own cocktail. "In layman's terms?"

"Strapless means without straps..."

"Okay, *that* much I figured out."

"Sweetheart neckline, is, you know," Riley drew a heart over her own chest. Brighton looked down at the motion. His eyes lingered for a moment before looking back up again. Riley blushed. She cleared her throat before continuing. "A-line skirt means that it flares out like an A. And tea-length means it's a little shorter."

"That sounds like something she'd pick," Brighton said. "Although to be honest, I thought she was going to get a gown that looked like Vanessa's, you know, the sea witch lady? Ursula's alter ego that tries to marry Prince Eric in *The Little Mermaid*? Have you seen that?"

"Yes!" Riley laughed. "It's my favorite Disney movie, which apparently is no longer the popular choice."

"It's Sierra's favorite movie," Brighton said. "Like of all-time, I think."

"*Favorite*, favorite or just favorite Disney?"

"*Favorite* favorite, I'm pretty sure," Brighton replied. "It means a lot to her."

"She mentioned that," Riley said. "That to her it was about belonging and rebirth and all that."

"And also, you know, I don't know how much she told you. But she was homeless for a little bit as a teenager," Brighton explained. Riley's smile dropped. What on earth? She had *not* mentioned that. Only that she had crappy parents. *How awful.* "There was one night where she couldn't find a place to stay and she just wanted somewhere safe to close her eyes. So she snuck into a theatre for a showing of *Little Mermaid.* She chose a 'stupid kid's movie' so she wouldn't be interested in watching and would just go to sleep. But she ended up loving it."

"How could she not?" Riley asked, wistfully. She imagined young Sierra sitting alone in that dark theatre, watching this fantastical story unfold in front of her. But then something struck her. "Wait, how old did you say she was?"

"She said she was sixteen when this happened."

Riley tried to do the math in her head. If Sierra was thirty-five, that made her six when that movie came out.

"That doesn't add up," Riley said.

"What doesn't?"

"Sierra wasn't a teenager when the movie first came out."

"She didn't say she saw it when it first came out," Brighton shrugged. "It was probably one of those special showings or something."

The waitress returned, eyeing Brighton's empty glass.

"Would you like another drink, sir?" she asked him.

"Sure," he replied, looking up at her for the first time. Riley watched as the waitress beamed, tossing her flaxen hair over her shoulder. It was clear she was attracted to Brighton by the way she looked at him.

Riley couldn't blame her. She knew Brighton was attractive. And he was more so when he was himself and not under Sierra's thumb. She watched as the server wrapped a hand around Brighton's strong shoulder, leaning in to look at the menu with him, directing him to sections of the menu where she thought he should choose his next drink, letting her beautiful glossy hair dip down onto the back of Brighton's neck.

A tiny hint of jealousy suddenly hit Riley.

She reasoned that it was for Sierra. That she felt defensive for her friend that a woman was touching her fiancé in this manner.

But Riley knew that wasn't it.

Riley felt insulted that this waitress felt no qualms about flirting with Brighton in front of her. It didn't mean that she was *interested* in Brighton or that she was laying any claim on him. She just didn't like the show of disrespect. She didn't like being overlooked and ignored as she often was.

She blinked.

The fury had collected so quickly that she felt embarrassed, even when no one knew her thoughts. She had begun her night angry that someone was watching her, and now angry that she was being disregarded? Had she gone insane?

It seemed like a particularly strange thing to think when she realized that Brighton's attention had been on her wholly as she let her mind wander. He didn't say anything. Just watched her. But it didn't feel unsettling. Though she thought it should.

Riley sipped from her drink, trying to distract herself from the strange sensation of being actively watched. She didn't have anything to say to break the silence. Nor did Brighton. The cocktail only drew his attention to her lips. Riley noticed him wetting his own as he continued to gaze at her.

Am I imagining this?

She cleared her throat, trying to make herself look bigger – more masculine. She spread her arms out around the armchair she sat in. Riley would have manspreaded in that moment if she wasn't wearing a mid-thigh tank dress. She was suddenly desperate to look...not like someone Brighton should be looking at that way.

The waitress returned quickly with Brighton's drink. It looked like something with whiskey. She explained its contents to Brighton, drawing his eyes away from Riley – finally. Riley watched as the waitress found every excuse to put her hands on him as she went on and on about a cocktail that only had five ingredients. What more was there to say really? Why wouldn't she back off? Her behavior was damn near predatory.

The possessiveness had returned.

She felt oddly protective of Brighton. She felt like he needed to be saved. The way she had needed to be saved from everything she was in now. She couldn't do anything about Sierra, but she could do something about this waitress. This waitress that somehow thought it was appropriate to *touch Brighton's hair.*

"Excuse me," Riley blurted out. The waitress froze, looking in her direction. Riley immediately doubted the interruption. Was she wrong to say something? Was she wrong to suspect something was going on? Was she now one of the many women in Brighton's life who insisted on calling the shots for him?

"Yes?" The waitress stood up straight now, removing her hand from Brighton's hair. She knew what she had done, but she wasn't about to admit it.

"If you don't mind, I was hoping to continue our conversation here," Riley said, icily. She wondered where this assertiveness had come from. Or was it aggressiveness? Had she skipped assertiveness altogether? Is this what weeks of fear, anger, and frustration created in her?

"Oh, of course, sorry," she replied, waving a hand as she walked off. Brighton turned to her, smirking. Knowing.

"My hero," he laughed, taking a *long* sip from his new drink.

"I feel like Sierra would've killed her if she saw that."

"Oh, for sure," Brighton nodded, eyebrows knitted together. "But that girl wouldn't have dared to talk to me at all if Sierra were here."

"And she dared with me? What, do I not look like I could be your girlfriend here?" Riley scoffed. Brighton arched an eyebrow. Being the ever-sensitive man he was, he seemed to have picked up on Riley's thoughts. He seemed awfully in tune with the way Riley felt, which served as further evidence that they had more alike than not.

"You're right," Brighton said, taking Riley's hand again. "That's actually pretty rude of her." He gave her hand a little tug, as if signaling for her to get up.

She did just that.

Then Brighton pulled her onto his lap.

She landed on top of him, startled by the sudden closeness and how quickly he was able to just *move* her entire body so effortlessly. Riley could smell the hint of patchouli, the whiskey. She could feel the hard muscles of his legs press up against her backside. He leaned his forehead against hers.

Riley tried to get up off of Brighton's lap, but he held her down tight. He tilted his head ever so slightly in the direction of where the waitress had walked off. With their foreheads still touching, she turned just a bit to look. The waitress was watching them now.

"You can't leave right away or it'll *look* like a lie," Brighton breathed.

Riley appreciated the ruse, smiling as she smoothed a hand over his chest. She swallowed hard, overwhelmed by the onslaught of sensations that had come over her.

It was nice to have her feelings validated for once. Nice to not feel crazy. She liked that she could relate to Brighton. That Brighton could relate to her.

But she couldn't help but think that Brighton had ulterior motives now. This wasn't like when he fed her a fry or some hug that lasted too long. Brighton's hands were now firmly in dangerous territory. She looked down, watching his strong hand moving from her knee to her mid-thigh, stopping just short of the hem of her dress.

"We don't have to be *that* convincing," Riley said, removing his hand from her leg and placing it on the armrest of his chair. "Besides, she can't even see us anymore." Riley tried again to push herself up off Brighton.

But he held her down once again.

She could feel a heat rush from her ears to her cheeks.

Brighton tipped her head up, and before she could move, his lips were on hers.

There was no mistaking what this was now.

There was *no* way she could explain this away.

30

To her horror, Riley found herself kissing Brighton back. The alcohol had kicked in on her end now, and she was slow to react. She couldn't pull away. Didn't want to. The kiss was at once electrifying and calming. She reveled in the dopamine rush, relaxing into his embrace and allowing him to pull her even closer.

It wasn't until his hand slipped up her dress that she jumped from his lap, snapping back into reality.

"Oh my God," Riley cried into her cupped hands.

She ran for the door, her palms still pressed to her lips. They burned, as if hell bent on reminding her of her indiscretions.

Out in the brisk cold, she was reminded of why she had gone out at all tonight. She wanted to lure her stalker out of hiding. To spot him once again. But she couldn't even care about that now.

Not after what she had just done.

She betrayed Sierra.

Betrayed...Gabriel...right?

What were you thinking? she thought. *What's gotten into you?*

Riley started to stride towards home, marching quickly in her sneakered feet before she rushed into a full on sprint.

Suddenly, the sound of a second pair of footsteps were behind her.

No. Not now.

Of course that stupid stalker would show up right when she was least ready to handle it.

She peered over her shoulder, catching a glimpse of just how far behind he was. Not far enough. In the moonlight, all she could see of him was the dark outline of his looming figure and the glint off the glass of...his thick black frames.

Brighton? No, Riley thought. *It can't be him. It couldn't be.*

But was it? Was he just coming after her to apologize or explain? *Was* it him and not the stalker? Or was he the same person who had been following her all along?

A cab turned onto the corner of Bergen and Smith. A woman stepped out onto the curb and the light atop the taxi switched on to indicate its availability. Riley jumped into the cab before the woman could even close the door.

Riley told the driver her address.

It felt strange now, to tell people she just met her address. Like it could be a danger.

She wondered how much of her life Brighton knew. She wondered what on earth he was doing following her around.

31

R ILEY: *Where are you?*
SIERRA: I'm at the studio, what's up?
RILEY: We need to talk. Are you alone there?

SIERRA AND BRIGHTON'S studio was about five times the size of Riley's office with ceilings twice as high. The floors were cement, unfinished. The walls were freshly plastered but unpainted. It was on the second floor of an old building that housed artists and crafters, woodworkers and metalworkers. And unlike Riley's unfinished office building, something about the aesthetic here felt deliberate and cool.

Brighton's corner had an assortment of tools and a mounted organizer with all his bits and drills, hammers and screws. A jigsaw machine sat below that.

Sierra's corner was just a long task table, wooden and polished so the surface was nice and smooth – definitely something Brighton had made. There was a sewing machine on one end, built into the table itself.

The space was vast and open with the exception of a small storage room and an adjacent bathroom. It was sun-drenched. An arched, south-facing factory window took up an entire wall and was lined with colorful plants that Riley just knew Sierra had planted herself.

For a brief moment, Riley imagined what it would be like staying friends with Sierra. She could practically see the two of them lounging on the oversized floor pillows by the plants, drinking tea with milk and eating scones with clotted cream and strawberry preserves.

Sierra held an embroidery hoop when she let Riley in, in the middle of what looked like an intricate, mosaic-like depiction of an elephant. In just a quick glance, she could tell that Sierra had more talent in her left pinky than Riley could ever hope to have.

She was sad to have to let this relationship go, but things had just gotten too weird. Between her suspicions of Sierra possibly hurting Brighton and the fact that she and Brighton had kissed...it was just too much. Riley swallowed hard, lamenting over the peek into a fun new life she now knew she couldn't have.

"I'm so sorry I haven't been more there for you," Sierra said, embracing Riley. She held her tight, holding Riley's head to her chest. The lump in her throat continued to grow. *Stop being so nice to me,* she thought. *I did something terrible to you.* Riley let Sierra continue to hold her despite the guilt that crept through her veins. She had to take comfort wherever she could now.

"It's fine, I really appreciate the flowers and the texts," Riley finally replied, pulling away. "There was so much to handle that everything you did was exactly the perfect amount." Sierra raised her eyebrows as her shoulders slumped forward in relief. It was like a weight had been lifted off her shoulders. Riley was surprised to see that she felt so bad. It made everything she was about to say even harder.

"So what brings you here today?" she asked. "Did I forget a vendor meeting? I know I'm not exactly the Type A sort of bride so whatever it is, I'm sorry I needed the reminder!"

"No, that's not it..." Riley began. *God,* could she do this? She stared at Sierra who stared right back, looking concerned. *If I didn't tell her, would Brighton? Should I just call off my work with them now? Should I just let Marco finish this job? What do I do?*

"Oh my God, I forgot the second payment installment, right?" Sierra asked. She hurried towards a metal desk that sat between her and Brighton's respective corners. "I only just realized I never got that to you. I'm so sorry."

"I...it's not..." Riley shook her head. She couldn't bring herself to say the words. Maybe she should just call off the job and let Brighton tell Sierra himself. She couldn't take a check from this woman. The job she had been doing was already shoddy considering all that had happened. And that was *before* she had kissed Sierra's fiancée.

Sierra took the check from her desk, waving it at Riley.

"See, it was here the whole time! I wasn't trying to skirt payment, I swear," she laughed nervously. "I'm sorry again. I don't want you to think that just because we're friends now that I'm the type to think it's okay to delay pay or something. I would never do that."

Riley willed the tears brimming in her eyes not to spill over. Could Sierra really be abusing Brighton? Was that why he had kissed Riley? Because he was desperate for a connection that didn't involve someone wielding their power over him?

She didn't want to believe that.

Riley liked Sierra. And not just because she was the first person to take genuine interest in being her friend. She felt energized around her. She felt genuinely cared for.

Besides, Brighton had said that Sierra was the one who ran off and was ignoring him. Riley knew now that couldn't be true, since Sierra was right here in the studio. She also knew now that Brighton was a liar, a philanderer. A creep. He was perhaps even the person who had been following her, though she still couldn't figure out what motive he had to do such a thing.

"Take it, silly," Sierra said, pressing the check into Riley's hand. Riley looked down, noticing for the first time how gnarled Sierra's hands looked. They were bony, veiny. Like they were on the wrong body.

To Riley's embarrassment, Sierra noticed her looking.

"It's awful, isn't it?" she asked, self-consciously retreating to rub her own hands.

"Oh, no," Riley lied. "I was just..." She wracked her brain for something to say. "...wondering if all that hand-embroidering hurts."

"That's why they look like this," Sierra said. "It's the price you pay for working with your hands for as long as I have."

Riley thought about Brighton's hands. They didn't look like Sierra's. They weren't bony and knotty and gnarled. But they were scratched up and bruised. Maybe he really was banged up because of their work.

The image of Brighton's hands on her suddenly flashed into her brain.

She gasped.

"What's wrong?" Sierra asked.

"I, um..." Riley couldn't hold it in. "I have to tell you something. I actually saw Brighton last night."

"Oh?" Sierra bit her lip. "I, uh...assume he told you we're kind of fighting."

"Yeah."

"Where did you see him?"

"He was at a bar on Smith. And he was really drunk," Riley continued. "And, um, I'm not totally sure how this happened, but he kissed me. That's why I came here. To tell you that."

"He kissed you?" Sierra's green eyes widened even more. Then she blinked. Several times. Her long eyelashes fluttered. "Was he okay?"

It was Riley's turn to widen her eyes.

That wasn't the first question she had expected to hear out of Sierra's mouth after her confession. It was strange. Sierra didn't even seem upset. She looked like she genuinely just wanted to know if her fiancé was okay.

God, they must really love each other. Had she really misinterpreted so much?

"He seemed fine," Riley stammered. "You're not upset?"

"I'm just glad he's okay," Sierra replied. "He ran off after our fight and he hasn't been answering any of my messages. I thought maybe he went up to Vermont. Do you know where he's staying?"

"I have no idea," Riley said. "Definitely not with me, if that's what you're asking."

"No, no, sweetheart," Sierra shook her head, reaching forward to grab Riley by the shoulders. "I know you would tell me if that was the case. Of course you would. After all, you came here to tell me about the kiss so I know I can trust you. Don't worry."

"Listen, Sierra, I'm really sorry about what happened. I wanted to come here today to tell you everything and that maybe it's best we continue with the wedding planning through Marco since it would be inappropriate for me to keep – "

"Oh honey, we don't have to do that," Sierra said. She pulled Riley in for another hug. "Thank you for telling me that he's okay. And I appreciate you telling me what he did. I hope it didn't alarm you or upset you too much."

"What – upset *me*?" Riley pulled away from Sierra. Was this woman a saint? After learning that her fiancé had kissed another woman, she was worried how that woman felt?

"It's a bit rude to kiss someone without asking first," Sierra replied. It was only then that she seemed to notice the shock on Riley's face. Sierra laughed, stroking Riley's hair. "Listen, I know it seems strange, but Brighton's just an affectionate man. It's something I've accepted about him. It doesn't mean anything. But you seem pretty shaken by it so I just want to apologize for him."

"I..." Riley stood there, stunned. "Okay, then." She didn't know what else to say.

"I feel so much better knowing he's okay!" Sierra exclaimed, covering her mouth as her eyes twinkled. "I just thought...God, I thought maybe something terrible had happened. I was barely holding it together just now."

"Really," Riley exhaled, still in a stupor. "You could've fooled me."

32

"No baby's breath. She'd rather have no fillers at all than baby's breaths – she was adamant about that."

Whether or not Riley was present, the world had been continuing on without her.

That much was clear as she stood in the busy workroom of Gail Thompson Floral where Gail herself was putting together a sample arrangement for Sierra's centerpieces.

Gail sighed heavily at Riley's command, plucking out the sprigs of baby's breath from the bunch of saffron calla lilies. She removed her red wireframe glasses from her face, allowing them to hang from the chain around her neck.

"I can just tell that this one's a problem client, am I right?" Gail huffed. "I hope she's fine with her scant centerpieces because I'm not giving her any other fillers or any more flowers with the budget you got here."

"That's fine," Riley smiled. It was nice to have someone talk to her without all the tiptoeing and coddling. Gail didn't know about Evan. Nor did she know just *how* much of a problem Sierra and Brighton had proven to be. Just not in the way she was thinking.

"Don't put my name on these then," Gail continued. "I don't want people thinking I'm sending out these skinny little bouquets because your generation has some sort of problem with baby's breath now."

There were whole blocks of hours now where Riley had forgotten about Evan's death, but in a way that was perhaps a little disconcerting. She had pushed herself to return to normalcy, and in doing so, she would momentarily fail to recall all that had preceded it.

In moments like this, while talking to the often combative Gail, Riley felt like she had been sent back to a time where she was still happily married to Evan. Where she'd return to her "home office" to finish up paperwork while he cooked her dinner and they'd talk about their work days like a normal couple.

But after leaving Gail's and remembering that she had an *actual* office to get back to, she'd be sent reeling back into her new reality with a force so strong that Riley often felt sick about it.

It was like multiple lifetimes had elapsed between her marriage with Evan and the life she lived now. But it had all happened in such a short period of time that Riley never got to adjust. She had been Happily Alone Riley, New Office Riley, Damsel in Distress Riley, Gabriel's Roommate Riley, and Riley the Widow. Now she felt like Homewrecker Riley, even if Sierra had tried to explain away Brighton's behavior.

A couple days later, Riley was informed via text that Brighton had returned and all was well. The wedding would proceed and everything would go as planned.

"There's no need to do anything differently," Sierra had said.

Meanwhile, Gabriel was still texting fairly regularly despite the fact that Riley continued to ignore it all. They were innocent messages, simply asking if Riley had yet to return to the office or if she was around for lunch. He was persistent, but seemingly cognizant of the space that Riley needed. He kept it to one text a day and never pressured her to reply. Perhaps he had taken note from Judy.

Her first day back at the office, Riley had rushed up the stairs, praying she wouldn't run into him. Though she was dying to hang out with Gabriel again like normal, she didn't feel ready. She didn't want him to witness any more of her messy self.

The next time she saw him, she wanted to be *normal.*

And it wasn't like normalcy *wasn't* returning. Her stalker had decided to take a step back, apparently. Riley no longer felt his presence or saw the flashes or shadows. Perhaps it was because she had actually scared him when she chased him out of that Duane Reade. Maybe she was more intimidating than she looked. It felt kind of nice to think that.

But with that worry aside, Riley was suddenly realizing how lonely she had been feeling. Having been exposed to so much socialization and then suddenly having it drop away was startling, like she was going through withdrawal.

So when Sierra invited Riley to join her and Brighton for dinner at their apartment, it was hard to say no.

It was still strange to Riley that Sierra was okay with what Brighton had done. It was clear now that Sierra and Brighton's relationship was perhaps equally unhealthy on both sides – Sierra being domineering when they were together, but Brighton being a cheater when he was on his own. Perhaps it was an agreement they had. Perhaps it was some kind of weird compromise that couples like them would come to as a way to keep things, *I don't know,* exciting?

It didn't make it any less weird to her.

Maybe it was just because Riley didn't get out a whole lot.

But clearing the air was something Riley wanted to do. They had continued work like normal, but they hadn't spoken in person since that day at the studio. There was no real way for Riley to gauge if everything really was okay or if she'd be able to act the way she used to around Brighton.

Riley had come so close to having her first true friends in Sierra and Brighton. Why'd they have to go and make things so complicated?

Still, Riley wanted desperately to make things work.

So she agreed.

~

SIERRA AND BRIGHTON'S apartment was well-decorated and surprisingly lived in for a place they hadn't even lived in for a year. It was nothing like their streamlined bare-boned studio space. Their furniture was mostly unfinished wood and appeared repurposed which was definitely Brighton's doing. But the look of it all was softened by the beautifully embroidered canvas draped over it which was definitely Sierra's doing.

Their home was a mirror of who they were as a couple – different, but complementary. Gorgeous on their own, perfect together.

But Riley knew now that they weren't so perfect. Riley knew that they fought, doubted each other, kissed other people. And so now it was strange to sit with them at their dining table, pretending like everything was okay as Sierra divvied up a vibrant salad dish that looked like modern art.

"It's radicchio, shaved Chioggia beets, and grilled peaches," Sierra explained.

"It's beautiful," Riley said, marveling at the colors in front of her. She had found it surprisingly easy to act somewhat normal around them when she was so fascinated by the beautiful things she was surrounded by. Riley shouldn't have been surprised by the picture perfectness of having dinner in their home. Of course people who looked the way they did would live and eat this way.

"Oh, it's no big deal. Just trying to use up the stuff leftover from my CSA box," Sierra shrugged.

Riley proceeded to eat, careful not to stain her lips with the highly pigmented dish before her. She looked up, self-consciously, to see again that Sierra and Brighton had no trouble navigating what she'd consider messy foods.

She caught sight of Brighton's lips as the prongs of his fork slipped between them. The cut had almost completely healed and no one would know it had ever been there if they weren't explicitly looking for it.

Riley suddenly blushed, remembering what his lips felt like. She knew how he tasted. She still remembered the feeling of his stubble against her skin.

The memory stuck with her hard, despite the fact that she was both drunk and fearful as she fled that night. He looked threatening as he chased her, but her perception had admittedly been poisoned by whomever it was that had been following her all this time.

And she was pretty sure now it couldn't be Brighton.

It seemed stupid she had considered that at all. There were 8.5 million people living in New York and half of that were men. Another good percentage would be roughly Brighton and Evan's height and there were enough people on the streets at any given moment that it simply *wasn't* unusual that Riley would occasionally feel someone else's presence.

Like that first time she had thought she was being followed, it wasn't even Evan. It was just some random guy who had as much of a right as she did to be walking alone at night.

But it was different with the man in the drug store. That much she still knew. He was like a textbook example of some shady creep with his trenchcoat and hat. And Brighton didn't seem to own a trench coat *or* hat. In fact, he never wore coats or hats at all. He seemed so perfectly temperate that his trusty flannel shirt was all that he needed.

It didn't make sense that he would put on some detective movie getup just to stalk Riley. And say he was actually attracted to Riley and had some weird need to know what she was up to at all times, it didn't make a whole lot of sense for him to skulk around looking for clues about her life when he could just as easily ask her. They had been alone together enough times. And he seemed more than comfortable with sharing intimate details about his life as well as *be* close to her. Physically.

"What's on your mind?" Sierra asked, smiling warmly at Riley as she ate quietly.

"I was just thinking how incredible this salad is," she replied. It wasn't a lie, exactly. It just wasn't the actual *predominant* thought she was having.

"You're almost done with your Riesling," Sierra noted, pointing at the single gulp of wine left in Riley's glass. "Brighton, top her off?"

"Sure," he said, getting up from the table and heading towards the fridge. Sierra turned to watch Brighton turn his back before huddling forward towards Riley.

"Did he apologize to you?" she whispered, looking concerned.

"What?" Riley whispered back. "No? When would he even have had a chance?" The three of them had been within eavesdropping vicinity the entire time Riley had been over. It wasn't like they lived in some mansion. It was just a generously sized one-bedroom with an open kitchen. If Brighton had apologized, there was no way Sierra would have missed it.

"I thought maybe he messaged you or something," Sierra shrugged. "I hope you're not uncomfortable."

"No, of course not," Riley lied. "You guys have been nothing but perfectly gracious hosts."

Brighton returned with the bottle of Riesling, pouring the remainder into Riley's glass.

"Oh, I don't want to take it all," Riley insisted. "I already probably had more than my fair share."

"We have another bottle," Sierra said, waving her hand like it was no big deal. "Besides, we already polished off a bottle of our own while we were cooking." She cleared her throat, setting her silverware down neatly on the placemats under their rustic ceramic plates. Sierra looked over at Brighton, willing him to look up at her. He did just that. "Brighton, was there something you wanted to say to Riley?"

"Oh, no, please," Riley protested. She did *not* need for this to happen. Especially not like this. This was about to be a humiliating experience for both Brighton *and* Riley. Brighton cracked his knuckles nervously, like he was a kid being reprimanded.

"Yeah, um," he cleared his throat, sitting up straight before looking at Riley. "About the other night..."

"Please don't," Riley said. "It was whatever it was and if we're all okay now, let's just not do this. Please."

"Well, you didn't want it to happen, right?" Sierra asked, arching an eyebrow as she tilted her head back a bit. "If you didn't consent to being kissed, then Brighton owes you an apology."

"I, you know," Riley stammered. "I didn't exactly fight it." Was this a trap? Was the whole point of this dinner to make Riley admit that she hadn't exactly pushed Brighton away?

"Really?" Sierra leaned forward onto her elbows, propping her pointy chin up as she studied Riley's reaction. Riley looked towards Brighton, as if for clues. Brighton looked just as shell shocked as he sat stiff in his chair. "Brighton, is that true?"

"I don't know," he muttered. "I was really drunk."

"And so was I," Riley blurted out. Would that really cover her? She wasn't drunk enough to do something she didn't want to do. She had kind of *wanted* to kiss Brighton in that moment.

"Guys, chill," Sierra laughed. "I already said that this was all just *fine*. I don't have a problem with what happened. And I'm actually really glad you guys are close now."

She got up, slinking slowly around the length of the dining table in her grey cotton maxi dress. Brighton's eyes were fixed on her. Riley could see him looking her up and down, checking her out as if this was the first time he had seen her.

Riley swallowed hard as she approached her. Sierra raked her hands through Riley's hair, pulling the hair tie off her ponytail as she played with the ends. Riley sat stiff, watching Brighton for any indication of what Sierra was doing behind her, outside of what she could feel on her own.

The sensation of Sierra's nails on her scalp felt oddly calming considering how on edge Riley was. She was more than a little tipsy as she continued to look at Brighton, hoping he would say something.

She knew he wouldn't though.

"Riley, you're such a pretty girl," Sierra said. "You should really show it off more often."

"Uh, thanks."

"You have such nice hair," she continued. "Doesn't she have such nice hair, Brighton?" Her voice was playful, but husky now as she directed her attention towards her fiancé.

"Yeah, it's very pretty," Brighton nodded.

"You guys don't have to do this," Riley said. She wasn't even really sure what they were doing, but she wanted it to stop. Now.

"You should be more confident, Riley," Sierra replied. "You have so much going for you. You're beautiful and kind and smart and talented. But you're not *confident* enough. You need to work on that."

"I agree," Riley squeaked. "We could all...be better in that department."

"Tell Riley what you like about her," Sierra commanded. Her hands were now resting gently on Riley's bare shoulders. Riley could see fear in Brighton's eyes as he looked up over Riley's head at whatever Sierra's face was doing.

"I, uh..." He blinked up at her. "What you said. She's smart and talented and kind."

"Tell *her*, not *me*," Sierra said, her voice harder now.

Brighton looked down, meeting Riley's eyes.

"You're smart, talented, and kind," he said. He almost sounded apologetic.

"And?"

"And beautiful," Brighton blurted out.

There was a pause before Sierra removed her hands from Riley's shoulders. She walked slowly, languidly towards the refrigerator and pulled out another bottle of wine. As she stood behind Brighton, expertly uncorking it, she hummed happily like nothing strange had happened.

Riley pleaded silently with Brighton. They were staring at each other now, both too frightened to look anywhere else. Brighton gave a quick, tiny shrug of his shoulders. His mouth hung slightly open as he shook his head.

"Let's say a toast," Sierra said, pouring Brighton a full glass of wine before giving herself the same. She set the bottle aside as she resumed her seat next to Brighton. "To this very special new friendship." She raised her glass, nodding at Riley to raise hers too.

Riley's hands were shaking. She was embarrassed about that, despite the fact that she was completely in the right to be shaken. She raised her glass, clinking it with Brighton's and Sierra's before drinking.

Sierra finished her full glass in a single breath. Then she pushed Brighton's glass away from his lips and kissed him. Hard.

Brighton inhaled sharply, struggling for air through the unexpected kiss. It was aggressive. Almost like Sierra was marking her territory.

But then she got up again, tugging on Riley's hand to bring her to the other side of the table. Then Sierra sat Riley down on Brighton's lap.

Her body felt boneless as Brighton's strong arms wrapped around her, keeping her steady in his embrace. Riley's head dipped back, but he caught her and she was thankful for that.

She blinked through the blurriness of her vision to see Brighton's face close to hers. His lips. Poor Brighton. He really was just like her. He really was defenseless against whatever Sierra's powers were over him.

Without thinking, she kissed him.

And he kissed her back.

It was just like that night at the bar. But when that was unexpected, something about this moment felt...premeditated. Even if Riley had technically made the first move.

She could feel his hands slip between her thighs, then up past the hem of her dress.

And she was fine with it.

RILEY WOKE UP, her body sore. She was naked.

And so was the body next to hers.

Brighton faced away from her, just as he had the morning she woke up with him in her bed. Except this time she was in *his* bed. Or rather, *their* bed.

But Sierra wasn't in the room.

It was just past midnight, just four hours since Riley's last real memory of that strange encounter at their dining table. Where was Sierra? The bedroom door was open and it didn't seem like anyone was outside. Where could Sierra have gone? What on earth was her deal? Was she some female version of a willing cuckold? Did that exist? Was Riley just some weird sexual game for them?

Oh God. They had slept together. She had slept with Brighton. She knew that much. She could feel it. She felt embarrassed, trapped under her sheets as she eyed the room for her clothes. Should Brighton wake up or Sierra return, Riley didn't want to be caught naked.

God, what is wrong with me? Her heart raced and her throat was clenched. She felt like she was going to be sick.

Why did she do this?

Why on earth did she do this?

She felt for Brighton, sure. She was sympathetic, or more accurately, empathetic. They shared a knowledge of what it felt like to be under someone's power. And at the dining table, they were both under Sierra's. But she couldn't figure out what could have possibly driven her to have sex with him. *Especially* if his wife-to-be was there.

But Sierra had to have been cool with it.

There was no way that she and Brighton could've done what they did if Sierra *wasn't* okay with it. And she was there last night. She practically orchestrated it. Riley remembered that. Sierra had watched as Brighton carried Riley into their bedroom.

And she was *fine* with it. In fact, she looked *happy.*

Brighton stirred, prompting Riley to jump out of the bed. She didn't want to deal with him awake. She didn't want to have that conversation.

She found her tank dress under Brighton's clothes. Her bra and underwear was nowhere to be found. *Whatever,* she thought. They could keep it as their perverted souvenir.

This was it. This was the last straw. There was no way they could work together now.

Riley dashed out the bedroom door, out of their apartment, and hopefully out of their lives.

33

T he two weeks following her bizarre sexual encounter, Riley became a total recluse.

　　She had enough trouble facing the world after Evan died, but after partaking in whatever weird fetishy thing Sierra and Brighton had roped her into, it felt as if anyone who looked at her could see the events of that night.

Riley did whatever work she *had* to do from her couch like she used to, except she made Marco stay at the office and do the *actual* bulk of it. She was overworking him for sure. She knew that.

Riley was shocked Sierra had the gall to continue contacting her, as if nothing had happened. But every message from her was just forwarded to Marco who had fully taken over their account without question. He was her gatekeeper now. The person who kept all the ignored people at bay. If it weren't for his constant, dutiful updates and fabricated excuses to all those who contacted Riley, she was sure that either Judy or Gabriel would've sent the police to break down her apartment door and drag her out.

If she could just close this bizarre, alternate reality chapter of her life, Riley would be *so* thrilled. But since every attempt she made only drew her deeper into further uncharted, outlandishly unsettling territory, Riley figured the only way to handle this was burn it all down.

First, she was going to let go of her apartment. The one she had shared with her emotionally abusive husband. Her ex-husband. No, her *late* husband. She didn't need *any* memories of Evan. She didn't need the memories of who she was with him. She didn't need to remember all those times he broke in, terrorized her, took from her. She didn't need to think about how his family blamed her for his death.

Riley wanted to shed *everyone* that knew her in that time. That witnessed those altercations. Maybe she'd even get rid of Marco – find him a new, better job and just go it alone from here on out. He'd also seen too much. Dealt with too much. Riley didn't need that guilt either.

She began with a single suitcase, throwing in as much of her clothes as possible. Then her toiletries. Her important documents.

Everything else could be sold, left behind.

Her heart was racing and her chest was heaving as she rushed around the apartment, stuffing things into yet another suitcase with shaky hands. She didn't even know where'd she go. Maybe just a hotel or an AirBnB for now. Or God, maybe it was time to run back to Judy with her tail between her legs.

Or Gabriel. Maybe...maybe she could just get over herself and be with him.

A sudden flicker of light came through her window and immediately, the flash triggered a deep feeling of dread and anger that she had come to know well.

Not again, she thought running to her windows and tearing open the curtains. *Not that I care anymore. This is going to end. This is all going to end.* She stared out at the direction of the flash, defiantly. She unlatched her window, pulling it up so that a roar of air came sweeping in.

"I know you're there!" Riley yelled. "I know you're fucking there so just show yourself!"

She knew that wouldn't work. It was just what was on her mind. It was just what she wanted him to do. What she had wanted to say.

Riley squinted, unsure if she saw anything at all anymore.

Her heart beat so hard she could feel it in her throat. She felt like she could choke on it.

Yes, she wanted to let go of everyone who ever knew her with Evan. But there was one person she could think of that would be hard to get rid of. Not just because he was permanently tied to her family, but because she missed him greatly. Because she really wanted, *needed* him to be by her side.

Even now. Especially now.

FOR WHAT FELT LIKE AN HOUR, Riley let Gabriel hold her in the pitch black of her apartment. She needed this. She didn't want to be in control of this moment. She wanted him to be. Someone who knew what he was doing. Someone who wasn't losing his damn mind.

Her breathing began to even as he cradled her. He sat between her two open suitcases, lights still off, not questioning what she was doing. Not saying anything at all. Gabriel could sense the priority was keeping Riley from crumbling completely, and he did just that.

"I need your help," she finally whispered. "And I need you to promise me that you won't think I'm crazy."

"I won't. Just talk to me."

"I'm being followed," Riley said, her voice hoarse. She untucked her head from beneath his strong jaw and looked up in time to see Gabriel furrow his brows, searching her face for answers.

"I...don't understand," Gabriel replied. "Didn't we figure it out that it was all Evan?"

"That's what I thought." Riley sat up, wringing her hands, hoping Gabriel would keep his promise of not thinking she was insane. "But it didn't stop. Not even after he died."

"How is that possible?" he asked. "Who do you think it could be?"

"I have no idea," she cried. "I just know it's a man. I saw him once.

I just know that was him. He was in a black trench coat and a hat. I know that sounds crazy like something from an old movie, but that's really how he was dressed."

"Are you sure he was following you?" Gabriel raised an eyebrow. Riley could see him wondering if she was a kook.

"I'm sure. I had my suspicions of who it was. I thought it was Evan...then someone else. But now I see that I was completely wrong about all of it."

"Did you see him tonight?"

"I think he's in the building across the street. Right now. I saw a flash. Like from a camera. And in the past, I've seen shadows moving in the window directly across from mine, even when it's well past when all the construction workers left."

"Jesus."

"I know I sound crazy, Gabriel," Riley said, desperation making her voice shrill. "But you have to believe me. I feel safe with you. I didn't want your help and I hate that I've swept you up into this, but you're the only person who can help me now. So will you?"

"Of course. Of course," Gabriel shook his head. "This is just a lot to take in."

As if the universe was finally ready to hand Riley her first assist, there was another flash from across the street.

"Oh my God, see!" she hissed. Gabriel's muscles were stiff, turning in the direction of the window as he remained seated on the ground.

"I did, yeah," Gabriel said. "He's gotta be the worst goddamn stalker if he's going to be that obvious." He crept towards the window, crouched low as he peeked between the curtains.

For two long breaths, Gabriel didn't say anything.

And then finally, his breath caught.

"You're right," he whispered. "There's someone there."

GABRIEL TURNED on the bedroom light, hoping it would trick their voyeur into thinking that Riley was in there.

Then, together, they snuck out of the apartment.

At first, Gabriel was insistent Riley didn't come with him. He was afraid of what they'd find, how dangerous it would be. He wanted someone to be able to report it if anything were to happen.

But Riley couldn't be left alone. Not right now. And the last thing she wanted was to send Gabriel off into his doom on his own.

The front door of the construction site was behind a plywood barrier, the makeshift door chained shut. There were clear signs that said, "DANGER" and "NO TRESPASSING," but they ignored it.

Riley's stomach did flips. She wondered if it was possible that they had both seen something that wasn't there. That they were now sneaking onto a dangerous construction site where there were an infinite number of possible injuries they could sustain. Maybe they'd fall in a hole. Have a steel beam hit their heads.

But Gabriel soldiered on, completely uninhibited. He allowed Riley to follow behind him as soon as he cleared the path with the flashlight that he brought with him. The lobby of the building was just about done. There appeared to be a working elevator where the car sat on the third floor.

The floor with the window that overlooked hers.

To Riley's surprise, the elevator dinged.

Gabriel and Riley froze, listening as the elevator doors opened three floors up. She could hear the footsteps stepping inside. Slow. Calm. Resolved.

As she listened to the elevator descend, Riley's heart raced so quickly she thought she would faint. Gabriel held onto her, as if he knew. She wished they had thought to bring a weapon of some sort.

The heavy sound of the elevator's mechanics settling on the ground floor boomed out in the empty lobby. Riley could see the crack of light between the elevator doors. And as soon as they opened, Gabriel pushed her aside, lunging for the figure that stood between them.

It was him.

The dark figure.

The man in the black hat and trench coat.

It was actually him.

And now Gabriel had him in a headlock as he wrestled him to the ground.

"What the fuck!" the man screamed. His voice was gruff. He sounded older. It was no one she recognized.

And in a second, he was flat on his back.

Gabriel pinned him down, making sure he couldn't get up.

"Who are you?" Gabriel roared into his face with an anger Riley didn't think he was capable of.

"Who are *you*?" the man yelled back. Riley stepped up closer, shining her own flashlight onto the man's face. He groaned at the light in his eyes, struggling to turn away.

The man was in his late forties, maybe. His face looked younger but he was greying and wrinkled. He looked harmless without that cloak of mystery.

But she didn't know who he was.

"Why have you been following Riley?" Gabriel asked.

"I'm not following anyone!" the man insisted. Gabriel picked him up by the shoulders and let him slam to the floor once again. The man groaned louder, grabbing at his shoulder.

"What's your name?" Gabriel asked. When the man hesitated, Gabriel tightened his grip on the man's arms.

"Paul!" he shrieked. "The name's Paul."

"Paul," Gabriel repeated, his voice sounding calmer but no less threatening. "Tell me, Paul. Why are you following Riley?"

"I was hired to," he managed to squeak.

"By Evan?" Gabriel asked.

"What? No!" Paul sputtered. "Evan's dead. I'm not getting a paycheck out of him." Riley wasn't sure if Paul was actually trying to joke around with that last statement. Either way, Gabriel wasn't having it.

It was then that Paul's eyesight apparently cleared enough that he could see Riley. He turned, looking right up at her, almost amazed.

Riley held his gaze, hoping Paul had any sort of humanity. If he did, he would spare her of any more of this and tell her how to end it.

She watched as his mouth quivered. Perhaps in fear. But Riley hoped it was in guilt.

"Tell me who hired you," Riley pleaded. Paul continued to stare at her, as if still stunned to see her up close for once, unobstructed. Riley felt her skin crawl. Who knows what this man had seen? Who knows how long she'd been followed?

"Your mother," Paul choked out. "It was your mother."

34

"How do we know he's not lying?" Gabriel asked, pulling the car out onto FDR Drive. They were on their way to Judy's house upstate. Riley couldn't wait another moment to speak to her. And considering the fact that Judy was not picking up her phone or returning her texts, this was the only solution she could think of.

"Why would he lie about that?" Riley cried. She felt so violated. She couldn't believe she had begun to trust Judy again, considered mending their relationship or even moving back upstate. Her mother had hired some random man to follow her. Some guy who called himself a private investigator. Why would she do this? What good did this do her? Was she really so desperate to keep tabs on Riley that she would send a potentially dangerous stranger to follow her around?

"Who knows," Gabriel said. "I just...he seemed so sketchy."

They had called the cops on Paul who confirmed that he was indeed a private investigator. They knew of him and weren't fans of him either, but admitted he hadn't actually done anything wrong.

"Why are you always so defensive of my mother?"

"I'm not," Gabriel insisted. "I'm just trying to understand. I know she's *your* mom and I believe you that she did all those crazy things when you were growing up. She told me some of it herself. But I know she regrets it and that she loves you. I just can't believe that she would actually do something like this."

"Neither can I, Gabriel," Riley said. "But I'm not *too* surprised. I should've known there was a reason why she was actually respecting the boundaries I had set for once. It's because she *knew* what I was up to all the time. That's why."

"This doesn't make sense though," Gabriel shook his head. "Why would she ask me to check up on you when she had someone tailing you this whole time?"

"She's greedy," Riley suggested. "I don't know! I don't freaking know anything anymore. My life is completely unrecognizable! My husband was *murdered* before I had a chance to divorce him. My job has become some sort of sick joke. I have no idea what's happening anymore!"

She let out a loud sob before falling forward into her cupped hands. Riley cried so hard she didn't recognize the sounds coming out of her mouth. Her chest heaved and her throat felt raw.

How would she ever recover from this?

IT WAS 8pm when they pulled up to Judy's house.

Riley hadn't been back in her childhood home since she was married. She didn't have great memories of the place and something about being there made her regress into the scared little girl she once was. It was like there was a spell on the house, one that Judy had cast to make Riley into the vulnerable, controllable kid she used to be.

Though Judy's car was in the garage and a light was on in the house, no one came to answer the door.

Riley had keys, but she didn't feel right just letting herself in. Not with how strained their relationship had been. She wanted to demonstrate to Judy what a normal, respectful distance meant.

But after five full minutes of waiting for her to answer and walking around the house to peek into the windows, Riley began to worry. It was unusual that her mom was unreachable like this. In fact, she realized this may very well be the first time.

Riley hadn't called enough in recent weeks to know if Judy's phone habits and patterns had changed.

Her hands were shaking as she tried to line the key up to the lock. Suddenly, she thought of all the awful things that might've happened. Maybe Judy had had a heart attack. Days ago. Maybe Paul wasn't just a private investigator but a con artist who preyed on old women. What if he killed her? What if his plans were to kill Riley too?

Finally, she managed to get the door open. Gabriel put a reassuring hand on her shoulder, pushing her gently into the house.

"Judy?" Gabriel called. Riley wasn't able to say a word. Her throat felt like it was closing up.

Nothing seemed too unusual. The lights were sometimes left on when Judy went out. It was her way of deterring potential intruders. But she usually left on something more obvious – like the living room light that was set on a timer, not the kitchen and bedroom lights.

"I'll look around for her," Gabriel said, leaving Riley alone downstairs.

Riley started in the foyer before carefully making her way into the living room. Everything looked exactly as it did when she was last there eight years ago. She could tell by the smell of baking that Judy had cooked very recently.

There was nothing unusual in the living room.

Then Riley made her way to the dining room. There was one plate out, one set of silverware. The plate had crumbs on it. Dirty. *That* was unusual. Judy never left things out overnight.

It was in the kitchen that Riley knew something had definitely happened.

The refrigerator had been pulled out of its nook, unplugged.

Behind the fridge was a small safe, about two feet by two feet – like the ones you got in hotels. The safe was open. Its contents were spilled out on the tiled floor.

Riley dropped to her knees, heart racing.

What was this? Was it money? Had someone tried to rob Judy?

"Gabriel?" she called, as loudly as she could. She didn't want to deal with this alone. She heard his heavy footsteps bounding down the stairs.

"She's not here," Gabriel said. Riley heard his footsteps slow as he entered the kitchen behind her. "What happened?"

"I don't know," Riley said. Her voice was shaking. "This was like this when I got here."

"What is all this?" Gabriel sat down on the floor beside her, inspecting the papers in front of them. They looked like a pile of miscellaneous documents. Forms, maybe. Paperwork.

Photos.

Riley picked up the first one that caught her eye. It was Judy and her father, Robert. The photo was faded, yellowing. Judy looked nine months pregnant – more than ready to pop. Robert was beaming as he kissed her belly.

"That's weird," Riley whispered.

"Why?" he asked, though he sounded distant, like his mind was elsewhere.

"My father died when my mom was just five months pregnant," she explained. "Here...doesn't she look...?"

"Riley," Gabriel interrupted, his voice grave. He had pulled a letter out of an envelope that read *My Dearest Judy*. "I think I just read something I wasn't supposed to."

"What?" She took the letter from him.

My Dearest Judy. The greatest love of my life. I know you'll hate me forever for what I have done, but it was only to spare you and our daughter from greater pain. I know it will hurt you now the most, now when it's fresh. I know it will hurt every time you think of me. But trust me that I know that this is best for all of us. I will never get over what I have done and I will never forgive myself. You shouldn't forgive me either. It was never your fault. It was always mine. And this now isn't your fault either. I need to go, before my self-destructive nature takes you with me. I love you. Know that.

35

"He killed himself?" Riley whispered. "Why?"

"It sounds like he was living with some sort of guilt," Gabriel said.

"But what?" Riley asked. "My whole life, I thought he died of a heart attack before I was born and now...now I know he killed himself?" She looked at the date on the letter. It was two weeks after she was born. "He killed himself knowing that he'd be leaving me alone with my mother. How could he do this?"

"Because he felt like he had no choice?" Gabriel said, looking unconvinced of his own words.

"Why would my mother lie to me?" Riley held the picture of her parents. They were happy. Gleaming. Glowing. They didn't look like a couple who would go through this. "She lied about how he died. She lied about me being premature."

"Wait, Riley," Gabriel took the photo from her hands. He flipped it over. "Look." He flipped the picture again to show Riley what was written on the back. A date was scribbled on it. A date that was a decade and a half before Riley was born.

Riley studied the photo again. That *was* Judy, right?

It was.

She looked a lot younger than forty in the photo. Because she was.

Oh my God.

Judy had been pregnant before.

Judy and Robert had had another child.

Riley had a sibling.

Gabriel pulled out a Polaroid from the pile. It was a picture of a redheaded little girl with a fishtail braid, about ten years old. She looked just the tiniest bit like Riley, but she could tell immediately that it wasn't her.

On the white part of the Polaroid was Judy's handwriting. *Jujube.*

"This..." Riley started. "This was what your mother called me. Jujube."

"I remember this girl," Gabriel said, squinting.

"What?" Riley asked. "How?"

"She's younger here, but she was my babysitter for awhile. I think I was like five or so at the time? She was a teenager. I only kind of vaguely remember her but I had no idea she was related to Judy."

Something clicked in Riley's brain.

"You had a crush on her," Riley said.

"Sure, I guess," Gabriel replied. "But you know, in a little kid way. How'd you know?"

"Your mom told me." Riley felt dizzy. She had a sister. Margaret had just about told her. Then Riley remembered something else. "Your mom said you asked about her once when you came home from college. Do you remember what she's talking about?"

"Yes..." Gabriel's expression suddenly darkened. "Oh my God."

"What?"

"God, I *never* knew *she* was Judy's daughter," Gabriel explained. "No one ever actually told me. I was just a kid. I just knew that she was my babysitter and that I really liked her. Then one day I had a new babysitter and I never saw her again. No one explained anything to me. My mom said it was because she..."

"*What?* She *what?*"

"She died."

Riley's heart sank.

"So that year I came home," Gabriel began. "Something had reminded me of her in school. I think a song or something she had introduced me to, I don't even remember what. But it reminded me that I had this babysitter I loved and I asked my mom where she went. And now that I was older, I guess she felt fine telling me the details. She said that the girl had run away one day. Then a few weeks later, they found her clothes washed up in the Hudson."

"That's why she was the way she was. The way she is," Riley said, tears brimming as she realized. "She had lost a daughter. So she wanted to keep an eye on me."

"What if..." Gabriel looked up at Riley, eyes wide. "What if she had never actually died? What if Judy hired that guy Paul to find her daughter and that idiot just went after the wrong one?"

"What do you think could've happened to her?" Riley asked. "What do you think my father had to do with it?"

Riley let her mind go to the darkest places. Had he hurt her? Did he kill himself because he had done something horrible to her?

If he had, Judy had to have reported it, right? She was a militant, responsible mom if not a compassionate one. There was no way she would hold onto the letter of a man who had killed her daughter.

Right?

36

R iley couldn't be in the house another minute.

She had packed all the relevant papers, letters, and photos into her purse and stood outside in the brisk cold of night, calling Judy. Again. And again.

And again.

The phone was no longer even ringing. It was just going straight to voicemail. Riley's hands were shaking. Her face felt numb. She knew that Judy wasn't going to be picking up, but she couldn't stop calling. She didn't know what else to do. She didn't even know where to begin to look for her mother.

"Riley, sweetheart?" a voice called. Riley's heart pounded at the sound of her name. She looked up, hoping it was Judy even though it sounded nothing like her.

"Over there," Gabriel said, pointing next door. Over the hedges was Mrs. Benson, their neighbor. Mrs. Benson's cherubic face was framed by a halo of frizzy grey hair. Riley walked over.

"Hi, Mrs. Benson, thank God!" Riley said, running around the hedges to meet her in her front yard. "I'm looking for my mother, have you seen her?"

"Yesterday, yes," Mrs. Benson replied. "I gave her a ride to the train station. She was on her way to the city to meet a friend. I would've thought she'd tell you so you wouldn't go through the trouble of coming up here! I haven't seen you in ages!"

"Did she say who the friend was?" Riley asked. Mrs. Benson frowned, searching her brain.

"Gosh, she told me but I can't recall," she muttered. "Is everything okay?"

"I just need to know who the friend was."

"Margaret!" Mrs. Benson exclaimed, proud to have figured it out. "She was going to see Margaret. Her best friend in the city."

"What?" Gabriel furrowed his brows. "When'd you say she left?"

"Well we were aiming to have her catch the 11am train which meant she must've gotten into the city around 2pm the latest," Mrs. Benson said.

"I would've been at work," Gabriel murmured. "I'll call Penny to see if she got there."

"What's going on, sweetheart?" Mrs. Benson said, looking at Riley with pleading eyes.

"I don't know," she replied, wishing it weren't true.

"Penny said she only dropped by to borrow a scarf because it was colder than she expected, but she was there," Gabriel said, handing his phone to Riley as he sped down the highway. "So she's definitely in the city."

"Where would she stay if not at your place?" Riley asked. "Who do you think she's with?"

"Penny said she was on her way to see another friend but didn't say who. We gotta find Paul," Gabriel said. "He's gonna know more than we do."

"How do we find him?" Riley scoffed. "I only got his first name and he's probably scared off of tailing me by now."

"We'll ask the police. They said they knew who he was."

37

"You think I'm going to give you *any* information after you assaulted me?" Paul's voice blasted through the Bluetooth speakers of Gabriel's car. Riley looked over at Gabriel. He gave a shrug, like, "ok, fair."

"We think Judy's in trouble," Gabriel said. "We need your help to figure out where she is."

"Listen, man," Paul sounded ballsier when he wasn't in the same room as Gabriel. "I don't know or care about what you're talking about. You're not paying me so I don't owe you anything. Contact me again and it'll be *my turn* to call the cops, hear me?"

Three low beeps poked through the speakers. Paul had hung up.

Riley and Gabriel sat parked outside their office building. They were back in Brooklyn but didn't know where to go next. The three-hour drive back was the longest hours she had ever lived.

So much had happened in the last few months. Her life had been turned upside down several times over. But what she had learned today had trumped *everything.*

She and her father had been alive together. He didn't die of a heart attack. Judy allowed Riley to believe that early heart attacks were in her bloodline. Let her believe that she was at risk her whole life. It had dictated so many decisions she made in her day to day. It was the image she always held of her father – a young, happy man who had looked forward to meeting her, but died tragically of a heart attack.

But no, he died at his own hands. He chose to take his life despite knowing Riley.

And it was because she wasn't even his first child. Riley wasn't the surprise miracle baby that Judy said she was. Everything she had ever believed about herself was a lie.

She was furious at Judy.

And not just because she had lied.

Because she was missing now and that meant Riley couldn't even talk to her about it. And because it forced Riley to worry for her. To feel sick over everything. And she hadn't even been missing for long enough for the police to take it seriously.

And as angry as she was, she had to admit her worry was what felt so much worse.

"Penny has to go," Gabriel said. "I gotta get back to her. I've already asked her to stay too late."

"Okay."

"You're coming with me," Gabriel said. "You shouldn't be alone right now."

"I…" Riley pinched the bridge of her nose. "I don't think I can just…sit right now. I need to find my mom. And you need to be with yours. So you should go home. And I should maybe look for help."

"I really don't think you should do that on your own. A lot of stuff just happened to you in a very short period of time. You've gotta be feeling pretty overwhelmed."

"Yeah, you think?" Riley scoffed. She regretted it immediately. She hadn't meant to lash out at him. Especially not after he had gone above and beyond to help her.

Gabriel looked at her, wide-eyed. He was as surprised as she was with her rude reaction.

"You want to be alone," Gabriel said, gruff. "Okay. Fine. I get it. Go be alone."

RILEY REALIZED her bracelet was missing.

The one her father made her.

The one that she always wore, no matter where she went. The one she played with when she was stressed out and *God,* she couldn't be *more* stressed out. She wanted it more than anything now that she knew what had really happened to him. It felt wrong not to have it in this very moment. Even if she were to learn that he had done something awful before killing himself and that he wasn't the ever-loving angel that Judy made him out to be, she wanted that metal chain around her wrist so she could decide for herself what would happen to it.

But she could barely remember when she had seen it last.

She searched the apartment high and low, tearing apart what was already a pretty disheveled looking living space. Riley didn't care anymore. She wanted that bracelet now. She wanted more clues about the family she thought she knew.

But she couldn't find it.

Where did I see it last? she wondered. It had actually been awhile since she felt the weight of it on her wrist.

And then it hit her.

No.

She had a vague memory of taking it off at Sierra and Brighton's.

So much for avoiding them forever.

There was nothing further Riley could do to find Judy at that second. But there *was* something she could do about finding her bracelet. There was something actionable.

She would find Judy, someway, somehow. But first, she needed that bracelet back.

38

R iley showed up unannounced, figuring a move like that should be fine considering what the three of them had been through together. The only thing she was really afraid of was being roped into another one their weird, kinky nights.

At first, it didn't sound like anyone was home. There were no footsteps, no music, no voices. But Riley saw a crack of light coming from under the front door and the shadows of someone moving around inside.

She pounded on the door again, feeling it vibrate against her fist and forearm.

She *needed* her bracelet. She desperately wanted that little piece of comfort while she was left to wonder where Judy could be.

Finally, the door opened. Sierra stared at her, surprised.

"Riley," she said. "Why didn't you call?"

"I was in the neighborhood so I thought I'd just, um, drop by."

"We've been texting you," Sierra continued. "You haven't responded so we thought maybe..."

"Yeah, um. I'm actually here because I think I left something that night."

"What was it?"

My sanity, among other things.

"A bracelet? It's a thick silver chain with a long pendant. Have you seen it?"

"I don't think so," Sierra said. She turned to look over her shoulder. "Brighton, have you seen a silver bracelet?"

It was then that Riley realized how strange it was that Sierra hadn't invited her in. Were they in the middle of something? Did they feel as awkward as she did about the other night?

Riley could make out Brighton's shoulder and left arm, sitting on the couch.

"No," he said. His voice was clipped. He didn't say or ask anything else. He wasn't curious who was at the door.

"May I come in?" Riley asked. She had a strange feeling about them in that moment. Brighton was speaking like he was being held hostage. "Maybe I can look around myself?"

"Um," Sierra hesitated. But then she opened the door completely and let Riley in.

Riley could feel something strange in the air. Sierra and Brighton were definitely acting weird. She wasn't sure if she should even bring up the other night. All she knew was that she wanted to find her bracelet.

"Where'd you last see it?" Brighton asked. He looked up at her briefly before shooting a glance at Sierra, and it was then she saw his eyes were bloodshot. There were scratches on his neck. His knuckles were bloodied and bruised.

Riley gulped. It would be hard to blame the clear, human fingernail marks were due to another work accident. She tried her best to avert her eyes.

"He and some of his buddies got drunk and roughhoused a little," Sierra said, as if she could tell what Riley was thinking.

"Oh," Riley nodded. She turned to face Brighton, trying to appear casual. "Did you win the fight?" She forced a smile. His eyes remained fixed on Sierra.

"Yeah, ha," he replied, his voice devoid of emotion.

Riley could feel a thickness in the air. It was the feeling of imminent danger. She was suddenly afraid. The way she was afraid when Evan was gearing up into his violent self. She had trained herself to recognize that shift, and she could feel it looming over her now, behind her. And the darkest of that dark energy emanated from Sierra's body.

"So, um," Riley's voice didn't sound nearly as stable as she had hoped. "I think I actually last saw it in the bedroom..." She felt odd finally acknowledging what had happened. Brighton looked down at his feet, rubbing the back of his neck awkwardly.

"Oh, right," Sierra replied, laughing a rather fake sounding laugh. "We had a bit of a night, didn't we?"

"Yeah..." Riley watched as Sierra walked over to the bedroom, opening the door.

"I didn't see any bracelet," Sierra said. "But you're welcome to take a look."

Riley felt nervous. She walked into the bedroom.

A rush of memories came over her.

The sound of their clothes coming off.

The feeling of Brighton's stubble against her neck as he lowered her to the bed.

Riley suddenly remembered something else.

She remembered Sierra's face at the door, watching. Then she had turned away and closed the door behind her. If there was some weird, cheating, sexual kink between them, Sierra hadn't stuck around to watch. At least not the entire time.

But it wasn't time to think about that now. She had many and *much* more pressing issues to resolve first.

"See anything?" Sierra asked. Riley looked up. She was standing in the doorway watching her, much like she had briefly that other night.

"No..." Riley said, truthfully. "I'm sorry I'm interrupting you like this, I just really need that bracelet. It means everything to me."

"Was it a gift?"

"Yes," Riley replied. "My father made it. He was a metalworker."

"Well, I'll make sure to keep an eye out for it," Sierra said. Her voice didn't sound sincere. In fact, she almost sounded disgusted. "If it means so much to you."

"Sure," Riley nodded. "Okay. Please let me know right away if you find it? I don't care what time of night it is, just let me know."

"Of course," Sierra replied, practically saccharine now. She held her hand out for Riley to take, but Riley couldn't.

Because she spotted something.

Not her bracelet.

It was Margaret's crazy, colorful muppet shawl. Just a small corner of it was protruding from Sierra and Brighton's closed closet, but it was unmistakably that silly scarf.

What was it doing here?

Riley knew it couldn't be just another similar shawl. That thing was one-of-a-kind in a way that was impossible to duplicate. It was the result of decades of scrap yarns knitted into one insane amalgamation of Margaret's creativity.

Judy had stopped by to borrow a scarf.

Penny mentioned that.

Oh my God.

She didn't have time to wonder how it got there. All she knew was that something was very wrong, that somehow her worlds had collided. She had to get the hell out of there. And the only way she could do that safely was if she acted like nothing was amiss.

"Well thank you for letting me bother you tonight," Riley laughed, stepping out of the bedroom and heading for the front door. "I'll let you two enjoy your night."

"Take care," Sierra said. Her voice was monotonous. Her eyes looked dead.

Riley let herself out, walking as quickly as she could without looking suspicious.

In the breeze of the night air, she picked up her pace.

She looked up at Sierra and Brighton's window. Sierra was staring down at her. She raised one hand. Wiggled her fingers.

Riley forced a smile, mirrored Sierra's wave.

Then her phone chimed.

She pulled it out.

A text.

BRIGHTON: Run.

RILEY REPLACED the phone in her purse, taking the longest possible steps she could without looking like she was running, just in case Sierra was still watching.

When she turned the corner, she made a full on sprint for the main road at the end of the block.

But it was too late.

Sierra was already bounding after her. Her long legs carried her farther and faster than Riley could ever hope to do.

And suddenly, she was on the ground.

39

R iley felt cold.

That was the first thing she noticed.

Then it was the fact that her wrists were bound behind her. Her ankles were tied together.

She opened her eyes, blinking into the darkness as her sight adjusted.

She was lying down on concrete, on her side. A pillow was propping her head up and Riley could feel the embroidery on the pillow cover pressing into her cheeks.

She was in Sierra and Brighton's studio. She could tell just by the view out the small window of what she suspected was the storage room. The moonlight was shining through, illuminating a figure sitting next to her.

Judy.

She was sitting upright, curled into fetal position. Her wrists were bound in front of her with clothesline, so tight that Riley could see it had turned her skin red, even in the dark.

The rope around her wrists extended down around her ankles. She was restricted to that fetal position. She couldn't move at all.

"Mom?" Riley whispered, worried she'd alert Sierra and Brighton outside. Riley could see Judy blinking slowly.

"Sweetheart," she whispered back. "You're awake."

"What are you doing here?" Riley's voice sounded like a whine as she tried to speak through her fear and attempt to be quiet. "How do you know Sierra?"

"Who?" Judy's voice sounded weak. Disoriented. Nothing like the authoritative, put-together person she was. Riley realized she had probably been drugged.

"Sierra, the woman who took you," Riley explained. "Is this all because of Paul?"

"Who?" Judy repeated.

Riley grew frustrated. What was this? What was going on? She wanted to shake her mother and force her to answer, even though she knew it wasn't Judy's fault that she had been drugged.

"Mom, you don't have to pretend anymore. I know you sent Paul to...I don't know. Maybe not for me. Maybe it was a mistake. You hired Paul to find Jujube. Right?"

Judy was quiet for a second. Riley could hear her sniffling.

"You know about Jujube?" Judy asked.

"Yes, I know. And I understand why you lied. And I understand now why you were the way you were and I want you to know that I get all that. And I forgive you." Riley could hear Judy full on crying now. "Please, please stop. They're going to hear us and we won't be able to talk anymore. I need to know why you lied about the way Dad died."

"I didn't want you to feel bad," Judy explained. "Everything I did was because I didn't want you to feel bad. I wanted you to have the life I couldn't give Jujube."

"I know that now," Riley said. "But why didn't you just tell me about her? I could've handled it. You let me believe I was an only child. You let me believe I was your miracle baby. That you were only able to give birth that one time."

"You *were* my miracle baby," Judy insisted.

"Why did dad kill himself? What did he do?"

The door opened with such violence that Riley and Judy screamed.

Brighton stood on the other side, staring down at the two women with a complete blankness.

"Who are you?" Judy cried. "Why have you taken us here?"

He bent down, picking Riley up off the ground.

"No!" Judy screamed. "No, please no!"

Riley could still hear her screaming as Brighton let the door shut behind them.

"What are you doing?" Riley asked. He didn't look at her. He didn't say a word.

He kicked open yet another door before setting her down on some cold tiles.

Then he left.

Riley sat against the wall, realizing now that she was in a bathroom. It was barebones, just another little room divided from the rest of the studio. There was a wide, porcelain sink, and beside it, a toilet.

Sitting on the closed lid was Sierra.

She was dressed unusually for her, in just an old, loose tank top and a pair of gym shorts. Her face looked tired. Her black hair was pulled into an unkempt ponytail behind her.

It was then that Riley noticed the scrapes on her knees, the scratches on her neck. Riley had definitely struggled before Sierra was able to take her.

"What are you doing, Sierra?" Riley asked. Sierra didn't look at her. "Why'd you take my mom too?"

Sierra remained silent before holding her fist out in front of her, right before Riley's face. She released her fingers one by one, dramatically, until a silver chain dropped from her fist and dangled from between her thumb and forefinger.

"My bracelet," Riley said.

"Nope," Sierra laughed. She tossed the bracelet at Riley. It skidded across the tiles. Where her bracelet should read Riley, this one read Jujube.

"I don't..." She was going to say she didn't understand, but then it her. Everything. All at once. "You...you're lying about your age. You're not thirty-five."

"Can't blame a girl for wanting to be young, right?" Sierra said, her voice teasing and singsong, as if they weren't in this bizarre scenario. As if they were just getting drinks during happy hour.

"You're Jujube," Riley breathed. "You're my sister."

40

"A whole decade," Riley scoffed. She felt bitter now. She had been duped a thousand times over. "God, you were really pushing it."

"You didn't notice," Sierra snapped. "No one did."

"You lied to Brighton this whole time?"

"He doesn't care how old I am," Sierra smirked. "Besides, he knows *everything* now and he's still with me."

"Shouldn't it matter a little?" Riley asked. "He wanted to have children with you."

"We can still have children."

"Not if you can't get pregnant."

"I can get pregnant just fine!" Sierra snapped.

Riley wasn't about to be sensitive with this topic anymore. Not when Sierra was a straight up psycho. Not when Sierra was Jujube.

"So what are you doing?" Riley asked. "What is all this? Why'd you kidnap our mother? What did she do to you?"

Riley suddenly recalled all the times Sierra complained about her parents. How hands off they were. How similar they were to Gabriel's parents. How much she hated it. It didn't sound anything like Judy, but Riley got it now. That method had failed with Jujube. Jujube ran away, for whatever reason, and never came back. So when Riley, her miracle baby happened, she vowed to do everything exactly the opposite manner.

"My mother is the reason we're all here," Sierra said. "She barely raised me. Barely wanted to. Then she turns around and treats you the way she did. Raised you to be tortured and scared. Drove you to a man like Evan and then left you in the dust."

"Can't you understand though? She was alone. She didn't know how to handle things. Yes, maybe she messed me up a little, but she didn't mean to. She just wanted to do things right and that's what she thought was right at the time. She didn't have our father to help."

"My father," Sierra scoffed. "He's just a bleeding heart martyr. He *chose* to leave my mother behind like a coward. He didn't have to. He just couldn't handle any *basic* obstacle in life. He couldn't handle a teenaged daughter who felt wayward and scared and needed guidance. He thought little trinkets like a bracelet could solve all our problems."

"What did he do to you?" Riley asked. "What did he feel so guilty about that he had to end his own life?"

"Hell if I know. He probably thought that it was something he could do to *redeem* himself," Sierra replied. "He drove me to leave. He called me lazy. He called me irresponsible. He called me stupid and heartless. I was only fifteen."

"That's awful," Riley said. "I'm so sorry he said those things." *Was that it? Was that all it was?* Was that really all it took to upset Sierra so much?

"I left that day," Sierra said. "I threw my clothes into the river hoping they'd think I was dead. So they'd never come looking for me. I wanted to start over. Without them."

"Why did you have to leave? Why did you do this? If they never hit you, they never hurt you physically, what was so urgent that you had to leave home?"

"You," Sierra said. Her voice was soft now as she looked at Riley. "Me leaving was your only chance for peace. If I had stayed, you would have grown up in a household in constant battle. You would have lived in a war zone. How was I to know that my father was so weak he'd go and off himself? How was I to know that my mother would snap, go insane, be someone I never knew her to be? I thought I was doing what was best for you. It was all I could offer you, don't you understand?"

Sierra sat down beside Riley, untying the rope around her wrists. Then, she handed her a tall water bottle.

"Drink," Sierra commanded.

"Why? What is this?"

"It's water," Sierra replied. Riley eyed her suspiciously. "I'm not lying, it's just water. You need to drink."

Riley didn't think she had a choice. She took a cautious sip. It tasted like normal spring water.

"Faster," Sierra said.

"Why?" Riley asked. "I'm not going to do it until you tell me why."

From the pocket of her gym shorts, Sierra pulled out a white stick. A pregnancy test.

The waistband of her shorts dipped when she retrieved it, just enough so that Riley could make out the glint of a scar across Sierra's flat belly. Sierra ran her fingers over it.

"See, I can get pregnant," Sierra replied. "And I can *stay* pregnant. But I had a little trouble, as you know. The miscarriage. The early birth."

Riley raised an eyebrow.

"You were so small..." Sierra said, choking up. "I felt so, *so* bad when I saw you like that. But I was too young. I kept hearing that it's good to have children when you're young but I was *too* young then. Too small. My hips were too narrow. I was too stressed out. I don't know what happened, but you came early. They had to cut you out of me. I was so scared."

It was as if the world had fallen away around them and Riley now existed in a total void, alone with Sierra. She watched as this beautiful, composed woman sobbed, kneeling on the ground beside Riley as if begging for forgiveness.

How could this woman be her mother? They were nothing alike.

They didn't look alike. Didn't act alike. Riley had more in common with Judy than she had with Sierra.

"I just want a second chance," Sierra continued, speaking into her folded hands as she slumped over her knees. "With you. With a new baby. This new baby I was supposed to have. But now it's too late. I missed my chance. It took me far too long to find someone like Brighton. Someone who listened to me and cared for me. Someone who wasn't some irresponsible druggie like *your* father was. But he was young too. Nineteen, I think. He knew he could take advantage of me and he did. And then he was just...gone."

Riley could see the glint of red and grey roots peeking out from Sierra's dark hair. Her real hair color. The red that she was born with. The grey that gave away her true age.

"Brighton was everything I wanted in a husband. Everything I knew would be the perfect father. He was willing to do things my way and I knew that my way was best now. I had a very long time to figure out what was right. But we waited too long. And we tried and tried and miscarriage after miscarriage, I realized it wasn't going to happen. But I wanted this. I wanted my second chance. We kept trying, but I also wanted to see you again. So I went looking for you. I sent Paul to find you and when I did, when I learned you were doing so well and you owned your own business and you were married, God, I felt *so proud.* Then I realized I had no reason to be proud. I had nothing to do with your success. You were whatever you were because of *my* mother. Because of how *she* raised you. Because as much as she may have made your life miserable, she didn't fail you the way she failed me. She got a second chance to do things right. Why couldn't I? I wanted that too. I wanted my own child, with my genes, my blood. And I wanted her to be perfect. The way I know we can be. The way we have yet to be."

Riley stared at the pregnancy test in Sierra's hands. She understood fully what had happened now.

"You wanted Brighton to get me pregnant," Riley said, choking on her words as she realized. Sierra probably knew that she hadn't been taking the pill thanks to Paul's constant surveillance. Or worse yet, maybe she was the one who had taken them. Maybe it was Sierra who had broken into the apartment that one time, and not Evan. "So that first night I woke up next to him...we had...we did..."

"It didn't stick though, did it?" Sierra laughed, scornfully.

"And Paul saw me buying tampons..." Riley felt sick. "So...so you tried again."

"Oh, c'mon. I could tell you liked him," Sierra said. "Brighton has that effect on women."

"You babysat Gabriel," Riley replied. "You knew him. You acted like you didn't. You acted like you didn't know me. You deceived all of us. Even Brighton. You control Brighton like he's your slave. You've brainwashed him. You treat him just like Evan treated me."

"You never thanked me for getting rid of Evan, by the way," Sierra replied. "And here I thought that was a pretty good gift."

"It was you..." Riley's jaw dropped. The surveillance footage had shown two men. That's what the police said. But Sierra was tall. In the right clothes with her hair covered, she could possibly be mistaken for a man in a grainy video. "You and Brighton..."

"We didn't mean to kill him," Sierra explained. "We just wanted to scare him off. Brighton, that man just doesn't know his own strength." The cuts and bruises on Brighton's hands. The black eye and the busted lip...those weren't from Sierra. They were from Evan.

"So why did you bring my mom here?" Riley asked, suddenly horrified.

"*My* mom. She's not *your* mom," Sierra said, sounding almost like a petulant child. She sighed. "Okay, so how do I explain this? Judy... Judy's kind of in the way of our plans."

"How?" Riley asked. "She didn't even know you were alive until you obviously told her to lure her out here. How did you even do it?"

"Oh, that was easy," Sierra said. "I had Paul call her. We pretended I was a psychiatrist and that I suspected my patient was potentially her missing daughter. I dangled all the right things in front of her – the nickname, Jujube. The right year I went missing. The pregnancy."

"She always held out hope you'd come back," Riley realized. That was why Judy was so tied to their upstate home. Why she wouldn't move back to the city, even when Riley did.

"Yeah, yeah, if she's such a great mother how did she let me get knocked up at fifteen?" Sierra scoffed. "She did bring me my bracelet though. And I have yours somewhere, I had it the whole time. Now we can match." Riley eyed Sierra, seeing how insane she truly was. She recalled again that day Gabriel asked her about wearing a white jumper to a messy dinner – whether that made her confident or just a risk-taker. Riley could see now that Sierra was neither. Sierra was just plain old crazy.

"What are you going to do to my...to *your* mother?" Riley asked. She knew the answer, but she had to hear it.

"Oh, you know. Put her out of her misery."

"She doesn't have to be miserable, Sierra," Riley said. "We can all live together, peacefully. We can work it out. It'll be fine."

"We can work it out, you and me," Sierra replied. "And the baby we're going to have. But Judy doesn't get to be a part of this picture."

"She's an elderly woman, Sierra," Riley said. "She's harmless. She couldn't possibly get in the way of..."

"What do you think she'd do when she learned you were pregnant? She'd have questions. She'd want to be involved. She would pretend like this was her first grandkid the way she pretended you *weren't* her grandkid. She'd continue the ruse and extend the lies into yet another generation of our family."

"How about me?" Riley asked. "How do I factor into this? How do I trust that you're not going to just take my child and leave?"

"I'm not going to do that," Sierra said, stroking Riley's hair. "No, of course I wouldn't, sweetheart. We would all do this together. The right way."

"And what would we tell the kid?" Riley asked. "Would we tell her the truth? Would that really be any better than a normal family?" It was just a hypothetical, but it suddenly dawned on Riley why Judy had lied. It was so much easier that way. So much better for Riley at the end – only because the other option was so much worse. Riley

208 AVERY LANE

had always hoped for a better life, not realizing she had already gotten the better of the two options she was presented with.

"Drink," Sierra said, her voice militant yet again.

"Sierra, we have to – "

"*Drink the water!*" Sierra shrieked. "Just drink!"

Riley did as she was told, afraid of what Sierra might do next. She wondered if it was possible that Brighton was in the other room, ready to kill Judy. She thought of all the power tools, all the means they had to dispose of her body.

Then she wondered if Sierra would eventually turn on her. She wondered if maybe Riley would eventually be another roadblock in Sierra's happy dream life. If Riley were to get pregnant, maybe Sierra would be the sweet version of herself only until Riley gave birth. Then she'd change her mind and dispose of Riley the way she would dispose of Judy.

That way she could have that child who shared both her and Brighton's blood. She could finally live that dream she had always wanted.

41

"May I have some privacy?" Riley asked when she finally felt like her bladder would burst.

"I changed your diapers," Sierra scoffed.

"Well, I'm an adult now and I can't pee with an audience," Riley replied. What she wanted to say was, "How many could you have actually changed when you ran off so soon after?" But her mind was still reeling and she was in survival mode now. She'd do what Sierra said, but she would try to maintain some sort of control. Anything that might mean she could get out of this alive.

Sierra rolled her eyes, getting up off the floor next to Riley before pulling her up with her. Riley's ankles were still bound.

"This is going to be hard to do with my legs like this," Riley said. She pulled at the rope, but it was knotted in some insane way that she couldn't get out of. She'd need a knife.

"Find a way," Sierra replied, turning away.

"Could you please...just step outside," Riley asked. "I'm going to need to maneuver in certain ways that won't be pretty. And I can't do that with you in here. You can stand by the door and leave it open if you have to."

Sierra huffed, but she did as she was asked.

Riley pulled her legs up onto the toilet seat, maneuvering in that ugly manner she knew she would have to so she could pee on that stupid stick.

Then she set it aside.

Riley wasn't sure what she would do if she was actually pregnant. She was pretty sure that if it turned up negative, Sierra would just usher her out to have sex with Brighton again. She shuddered at the thought.

She thought about Gabriel. And Margaret.

Margaret who had inadvertently given her the first clues she needed to learn that her whole life was a lie. Sierra claimed she didn't feel loved by her family which was why she was forced to run into the arms of another young boy. But Margaret had taught her father how to fishtail Sierra's hair. And it actually happened, as evidenced by the photo Riley found.

Why was Sierra incapable of seeing the love that was there?

"Our dad..." Riley started. "Or, well, your dad...what was he like?"

Sierra's back was still to her, but Riley could see that she had flinched.

"He loved his work," Sierra replied. "He spent all day in the metal shop. He loved his wife. It was like they loved each other too much to have time to love me."

"What made you feel that way?" Riley was trying to be empathetic. To ask questions without sounding like she was contradicting Sierra.

"My friends' parents...they were involved in their lives. They suggested sports and piano lessons and playdates. They had an opinion on what they should do. Judy and Robert just thought they knew better than all the other suburban parents. They were so sure of themselves and their free-range children theory that they just...let me flounder."

Like Margaret and Teddy did with Gabriel.

But Gabriel wasn't resentful like Sierra was. Gabriel and his brothers turned out fine.

And Riley was still pretty sure she would've flourished with that sort of freedom just as well.

"They thought they knew everything..." Sierra continued. "They let me drink, hang out with older kids. And then they were *so shocked* when I ended up pregnant. Like it was my fault. Like they hadn't put me in that position."

Riley suddenly remembered the pregnancy test.

She looked down.

Negative.

It was negative.

She didn't know what this meant for her. She didn't know what to tell Sierra. She wanted to let Sierra ramble on about her childhood because...because she was pretty sure she'd be forced to have sex with Brighton if she told Sierra it was negative.

And there was no way her child belonged in *this* world. There was no way Riley would let that happen.

"That sounds awful," Riley said. She sounded genuine, because she was. Riley remembered what she was like at fifteen. She was still a child. And Sierra dealt with a pregnancy at that age? Riley couldn't imagine it. "That must've been really hard."

Riley gripped the pregnancy test in her fist. She remembered something.

This wasn't the first time Riley had taken a pregnancy test.

The first time she did was with Mindy.

Mindy was the one who thought she was pregnant. Riley, at the time, hadn't even had sex yet. But Mindy didn't want to take the test alone and so in a silly attempt at solidarity, Riley offered to do it with her.

They both sat in front of their pregnancy tests, waiting for the results.

Mindy's was negative. She rejoiced.

Riley left hers alone, sitting on the sink while they happily downed a box of doughnuts to celebrate.

When Riley returned to the bathroom to wash the powdered sugar off her hands, she noticed that her pregnancy test read positive.

She knew she wasn't pregnant. She hadn't done what she needed to do to *get* pregnant.

Which is how she learned that leaving *any* pregnancy test around for that long meant it would eventually show a positive sign.

She had to keep Sierra talking.

"How'd you pick your new name?" Riley asked.

Sierra was quiet, as if she was considering if she wanted to share the story. She looked over her shoulder at Riley. Her eyes were shiny.

"The way I picked yours," Sierra replied. "I bought a book. At a drug store. And I chose something I thought was pretty. I was really excited about it. Riley. When I left home, I took the book with me. One of the only things I took with me. I knew I'd need a new name if I didn't want them to find me. It took me forever to settle on something, but then...I saw *The Little Mermaid*." She laughed at herself. "Vanessa looked like Ariel with dark hair. My hair was red. I liked the dark hair. So I dyed it black. And that night when I flipped through the baby name book, I noticed the name Sierra. Which meant dark. Like my new hair. I liked that."

Her reasoning was so childlike, exactly the way Riley envisioned a teenager's thought process in such a situation. Sierra was stunted. It was no wonder she tried to turn back the clock.

"Why'd you change your age?" Riley asked. Sierra turned completely towards her now, leaning against the doorframe.

"Because I could," Sierra replied. "I looked young. I knew that because I was constantly being hit on by much younger guys and getting carded still. So I went with it. Even better, I thought. I'd buy myself ten years. Over time, I started to believe I was the age I said I was. Until Brighton and I tried to conceive. And I was told that thirty-five was 'geriatric.' I remembered my own secret then. That even if I looked the part on the outside, I was no longer that way on the inside. And even my fake age was too old to have kids now."

Riley took a discreet peek at the pregnancy test. The negative sign was slowly being joined by a perpendicular line. It was working. The extra time elapsed was giving a false positive. She just needed a little while more.

"You have a kid though," Riley said, her voice shaking. She was about to embark on something risky. "I'm your daughter. Just because you couldn't be my mother on the outside, you were always, by blood, by genetics, by every definition – you're my mother. You always were."

"But I wasn't *there* for you," Sierra replied. "I'm a hypocrite."

"You did what you needed to do, like you said," Riley insisted. "You did the right thing. It just didn't turn out like you hoped. And now that everything's out, now that there are no more secrets, we can do this right. Like you said. Look." She held the pregnancy test out to Sierra. It read positive now. A big fat plus sign. Clear as day.

Sierra took the test from her, staring at the plus sign with wide, hopeful eyes.

"Oh my God," she whispered.

"Should we tell Brighton?" Riley asked.

"He's in the middle of something right now..." Sierra replied. Riley's stomach lurched.

"Wh – what is he doing?" Riley swallowed hard, hoping to God Judy was still alive.

"He's just...I don't know," Sierra said, still looking at the pregnancy stick in awe. Through the crack of the door, Riley could see the glint of something. There was a scraping noise. She was pretty sure Brighton was sharpening a knife.

"What's he doing?" Riley insisted on knowing. She had to. She had a right to know now, right? Now that she was carrying their child?

"Don't worry about it," Sierra said. She was smiling now. A real, genuine smile. "Let's get you out of that rope." Sierra grabbed a hold of Riley by the waist, lifting her up off the ground and dragging her out to Brighton.

Sierra set Riley down on a stool by Brighton's metal task table. She grabbed a box-cutter, switching it open and cutting at the rope around Riley's ankles, gently.

The movement distracted Brighton. He turned around, and it was then that Riley saw for *sure* that he was sharpening a knife. Her heart stopped.

Brighton's eyes looked weary. His good looks were suffering under the weight of their circumstances. He looked at Riley, apologetically. His broad shoulders were slumped, defeated. He was a cog in all this. Just a cog. He was too weak to break away.

"Riley has some news to share," Sierra said. She sounded chipper, like she was referring to a six-year-old who had just lost her first tooth. "Right, Riley?"

"Um, yeah," she replied.

"Go ahead. Tell him."

Riley looked up at Brighton. He raised a tired eyebrow, remaining quiet.

"I'm pregnant," she replied.

The statement woke Brighton up.

He looked horrified. But it only lasted a second before Sierra was standing again, facing him. The horror was quickly replaced by a big, fake smile.

"Oh my God!" he exclaimed, sounding almost convincing. He hugged Sierra tight. Brighton looked up at Riley, his eyes back to fear. *I'm sorry,* he mouthed to her.

"We're going to be parents," Sierra cried. "Finally."

For all her talk about doing things right, Sierra was sure getting off on a weird start. Riley didn't know what she could do next or what this meant for her life. Was the wedding still happening? Would she have to fake her way through that event?

Could she maybe leverage her "pregnancy" now to save Judy's life?

42

"We should celebrate, right?" Riley asked.

Brighton was still holding Sierra, watching Riley's expression over her shoulder. He narrowed his eyes at her, trying to figure out what was going on – what she was thinking. Sierra let go of him, rushing towards a shelf full of miscellaneous tools and knick-knacks.

When she turned around, she was holding a Polaroid camera.

"This was one of the other things I took with me from home," Sierra explained.

"And the bracelet too?" Riley asked.

"No," Sierra scoffed. "That was in the pocket of my jeans that I threw in the river. I can't believe they managed to hold onto it. Judy actually brought it today thinking we were going to have some *wonderful* reunion."

Riley felt her heart break for Judy. She had no idea of the trap that awaited for her.

"Did you send me that message?" Riley asked. "That Polaroid under my door saying that we're never really alone?"

Sierra looked up at Riley.

"Of course," she replied, as if it were perfectly normal. "I wanted you to know that I'll always be with you." Riley almost wanted to laugh. *That's* how she meant it? If she needed further confirmation that Sierra was bat shit insane, this was it.

"And the flowers?" Riley looked at her, wide-eyed.

"The what?" Sierra muttered, her focus on setting up the camera. *Okay, I guess that was Evan,* Riley thought, shaking her head. And this whole time Riley thought she was being terrorized by just *one* person. She should've known that was too much effort for any single individual, no matter how crazy they were. "Okay. Smile for the camera, sweetie." She held the camera up, looking through the viewfinder to see what Riley knew was a totally confused expression on her face.

"Why are you taking a picture?" she asked.

"We're celebrating," Sierra said, matter-of-factly. "So we should remember this day." *Why on earth would you want to remember this day?* Riley thought, incredulous. But she fought her urge to say it. There was no sense in reasoning with crazy people. Besides, Sierra probably thought that just the conception of their *collective* child was actually worth commemorating.

She looked into the viewfinder again, but didn't snap the picture. Instead, she lowered the camera, frowning, looking at Riley and then Brighton before shrugging her shoulders.

"This doesn't look like a celebration," Sierra said. *Oh, you think?!* Riley thought. This probably looked every bit the hostage situation it was. "What do you think could help?" Brighton looked over at Riley, his eyes pleading for answers. But she had nothing. She had hoped he did.

"Cake, maybe?" Riley finally said.

"Yes! Of course. What kind of cake?" Sierra asked, nodding at the suggestion. "Anything you want, I'll get it for you. Any flavor. Oh, this is going to be incredible. I can make it all up to you now! I can finally give you everything I couldn't give you back then."

Riley wondered if she could just cut to the chase. If she could just ask Sierra to let Judy go. But something told her to proceed carefully.

"Um, do you know where my phone is?" Riley asked. She could definitely use her phone. She could text Gabriel. "We can order some delivery. From my favorite bakery. This place on Smith, I don't know if you've tried it..."

"I can order for us," Sierra said. "Just tell me what you want." *Nope, that didn't work.*

"Or why don't we just go out?" Brighton suggested. "That'd be nice, right? I mean, this is our workplace. Who celebrates at work?"

Sierra was quiet. Riley wondered what was going through her head. Did she suspect something was going on? Could she detect the disingenuous nature of Riley's request? Was she suspicious of all the words Brighton had just blurted out?

"Do you want to go out, Riley?" Sierra asked.

Riley didn't know.

Was it safer to go out? Safer to stay?

Definitely safer to go out, right?

But it would only be safer for Riley. She could flag down a stranger to help her, but she couldn't ensure that Judy would be okay alone in that dark room. She had been drugged. She was cold. Dehydrated. Who knows how she'd fare in there?

Riley needed to tell Gabriel. She needed someone to know where Judy was so that they could help her.

But how?

There was a loud rap at the door.

Riley gasped, unable to hide her nerves. The sound had shaken her thoroughly. Sierra didn't look surprised. She was expecting someone.

She walked over, unlatching the giant padlock and sliding open the metal door.

Paul walked in.

"Give me a second," Sierra said. "I haven't actually had a chance to write it out yet."

Paul eyed Riley from across the room, looking a little confused.

"What was the balance?" Riley asked, hunched over her checkbook.

"Uh, here," Paul took a folded piece of paper out of his trench coat, handing it to Sierra.

He seemed to sense that something was amiss. Maybe because he had realized that Riley shouldn't be there. Not when she had just called earlier, suspicious of the person who had hired Paul.

Riley hoped to God he was smart enough to put two and two together. And if he was smart enough, Riley hoped he was a better person than he initially appeared. Maybe he would do the right thing now. Maybe he'd call the police. Something. Anything.

BUT HE DIDN'T. Paul took the check. Paul left.

And that was that.

"So? Riley? What do you think?" Sierra asked.

Riley stood stunned, not knowing what to say. She had just watched her chance to escape walk out the door.

"Um, let's go out," she blurted out. "That sounds nice."

"Brighton, you want to stay behind?" Sierra asked.

"Why?" he asked.

"To handle anything that might need to be handled," she said, her voice cold.

"I think – I think we can probably leave for a bit and be fine," Brighton replied. He probably knew what he would be expected to do while they were away. He was probably too weak-willed to just let Judy go by himself. Or maybe he needed more time with Riley so he could understand how to help.

"What's the sense of celebrating without the father?" Riley laughed nervously. The question proved to be a fatal error. Suddenly, Sierra knew something was up.

"Let's just order something," Sierra said, definitively. Riley tried not to show her disappointment.

"Sure, that sounds good," Riley replied, trying to remain unsuspicious. Sierra was eyeing her now, as if trying to figure out if this act was for real. Riley couldn't blame her. She was a terrible actress. She always had been.

She felt faint now.

This was a disaster.

It was a disaster on its own but Riley having no clue how to handle it, Brighton being too meek to do anything, Sierra being as sharp as she was – this made it an utter and *complete* disaster.

Her vision began to cloud.

She fanned herself, blinking, willing herself not to pass out.

"Riley?" Sierra said. Her voice was concerned now. She knew *this* wasn't fake.

"I..." Riley climbed down from the stool. "I feel a little..." She steadied herself on the task table. *Oh God,* she thought. *What wonderful timing.*

Riley tipped her head forward, leaning her forehead against her folded arms. She could feel Sierra stroking her hair, stroking her back. She seemed gentle now. Sweet.

"The first trimester was rough on me," Sierra said. "We might have to expect the same for you."

Riley could feel the blood rushing back to her head. She opened her eyes. The metal of the task table came into clear focus. She didn't feel faint anymore.

But she wasn't about to say anything.

Not when she managed to get Sierra in this position.

Riley let her knees buckle, crumpling to the ground.

"Riley!" Sierra yelled, cradling Riley's head on her lap. "Riley? Can you hear me?"

Yeah, you're screaming in my ear, Riley thought. But she remained still.

She wasn't sure where this was going to get her, but it was going to buy her time. Sierra wanted to protect her assets. The unborn child she thought actually existed.

"Brighton, will you take her to the couch?" Sierra asked. Her voice was soft and submissive now. Riley could tell it wasn't to manipulate Brighton. She was actually worried. A pang of sadness struck Riley's heart, despite herself.

"The couch?" Brighton asked. "You mean the one in the room..."

"That's the only one, isn't it?" Sierra's voice was biting again, icy. Riley almost shivered under the sudden callousness. *Poor Brighton.*

"Okay," Brighton said.

Riley could feel him scoop her into his arms. She tried to remain limp and convincing. But it was hard when her mind was racing. What was her next step? She hadn't even thought it out. Once she was in the room with Judy, what would she do? Throw herself over her? Beg? What good could she do in that room?

Brighton walked her over. She could hear the doorknob turn.

There was a rush of wind where there wasn't before.

Riley heard Brighton grunt as he fell backwards. Riley tumbled down with him.

She opened her eyes, pushing herself up to see Gabriel standing in the doorway of the room where Judy had been.

How on earth...?

Gabriel grabbed Brighton by the collar, throwing another fist into his face. The fall had knocked the wind out of her. She wanted to tell Gabriel to stop, that Brighton wasn't the real threat.

But then Brighton gained his bearings. Though he wasn't as big as Gabriel, he apparently made a decent match. Gabriel was somehow on the floor now, Brighton pinning him down by the chest.

They tumbled, several times, back and forth – each gaining the upper hand just seconds after the one before.

Then finally, Gabriel got Brighton down for just a bit longer. Riley could see Gabriel had him by the throat.

"Gabriel, no!" she exclaimed. He could kill Brighton. Easily. Riley knew this.

Her cry served as exactly the distraction that would make Gabriel lose the fight completely. He looked up in Riley's direction, distracted for just long enough that Sierra was able to plunge the freshly sharpened knife into his shoulder.

"No!" Riley shot to her feet, darting towards Gabriel. Sierra had just done to him what she had planned on doing to Judy. Riley threw her tiny body over Gabriel's back.

Just in time to receive the second swing of the knife.

The knife was so sharp, it cut through Riley's arm like she was air – like, she was nothing at all. She could feel Sierra catch herself, hesitate just enough so that the knife didn't go all the way through. But her reflexes weren't enough.

Riley couldn't even scream.

The shock had taken over. She watched as Sierra pulled the knife back out and threw it aside.

"No!" she cried. "No, no, no! Brighton!" Sierra's eyes looked wild. She looked up for Brighton. "Get something to stop the bleeding! Anything!"

Brighton grabbed the roll of canvas that Sierra had by her embroidery. He tore into them, handing strips of it to Sierra who quickly wrapped them around Riley's wound.

Riley's vision was fading again. She looked over at Gabriel. He was still moving, groaning in agony.

"We have to take them to the hospital," Brighton pleaded. "You got him pretty bad. And Riley – she's – how is this going to affect the baby?"

"And what do we tell them?" Sierra seethed. "That I stabbed them?"

"I was breaking and entering," Gabriel grunted in desperation, his breathing rapid and wheezy. "You had reason to attack. Just tell them that." He was trying to pull himself up, but the wound in his back had his muscles haywired. He collapsed again, breathing shallower now.

"Gabriel," Riley said. Her voice was weak. Breathy in a way that made her concerned. She still barely felt any pain, but something didn't feel right. "Gabriel, where's my mom?"

"She's fine," he rasped. "I got her. Don't worry."

"I'm sorry, Riley. I'm so sorry," Sierra cried. She cradled Riley in her lap, stroking her hair. Riley could feel Sierra's tears falling on her. She could feel the vibration of her body as the sobs ripped through Sierra's chest.

Then everything went black.

43

R iley woke up to the same sensation she had felt when she lost consciousness.

Someone stroking her hair.

She opened her eyes to find Judy sitting on the hospital bed. The slightest smile spread on her face when their eyes met.

"You're going to be okay," Judy said. "Everything will be fine."

"Mom," Riley managed to force out of her throat.

"I thought I was going to lose you," she replied.

"You always think you're going to lose me," Riley joked. She hoped Judy was in the mood to receive it. To her relief, Judy laughed.

"This isn't the same, Riley! You were just stabbed!" Judy guffawed. It was weird to hear her say those words in such a jovial manner. "But you're going to be okay. The doctor said everything will heal nicely." Judy bit down hard on her trembling lip, looking skyward as she tried to will the tears back into her eyes.

"What?" Riley asked, frightened. "Is it Gabriel? Is he okay?"

"Yes," Judy whispered. "He'll be fine too."

"So I'll be fine and he'll be fine. Then what is it?"

"When you were born, we weren't sure you'd make it," Judy said. "But you did. Because you've always been so, *so* strong. But then

Jujube left. And I lost your father. After all that, I just couldn't see that anymore. I thought you were some fragile, porcelain doll that I had to protect with all my might. Not because you weren't strong enough, but because I wasn't strong enough. Because I didn't know how to raise you with the truth."

"I understand," Riley said, nodding. "Please don't cry, Mom. I really do understand now."

"I hope you can forgive me."

"There's nothing to forgive. We do what we think is right at the time. We never know how it'll turn out. But if you just told me...I could have helped you," Riley said. She cleared her throat in an attempt to sound stronger, to reassure Judy. "I could have helped you," she repeated. It sounded convincing this time. "If I had known what made you this way, I would have understood better. We could have gone through it together."

"I couldn't burden you with it, Riley. I didn't want you to somehow think it was your fault what happened to Jujube and what happened to Dad. I was afraid that's what it would look like if I told you."

Riley wanted to say something, but there was nothing to say. It had all been done. It was all in the past now. The truth was out there but it didn't change the way that any of them had led their lives.

Judy ended up where she was.

Riley ended up where she was.

And Jujube became Sierra.

"How exactly is Gabriel doing?" Riley asked. "It looked so bad, Mom. It looked really, *really* bad."

"He's *really* okay," Judy insisted. "The doctor said it was a subcutaneous wound. It didn't hit anything that would do permanent damage, luckily. I'm not sure it would've been the same if he didn't have all that excess muscle."

"Excess muscle," Riley muttered, laughing just a bit. "And how did he get you out? How did he know where we were?"

"You'll have to talk to him yourself," Judy said. "All I know is that he climbed up through the window and got me. Then he used the same rope Brighton used to tie me up and climbed back out with me on his back. It was terrifying, but we somehow made it."

"He left Margaret alone at home?"

"No," Judy chuckled, shaking her head. "She was in the car when he put me in there! The man brought his elderly mother on a rescue mission. He must have been pretty confident he'd be coming back."

"I wasn't," Riley said. "I wasn't confident any of us were going to make it."

"I was so frightened in the car alone with Margaret," Judy explained. "I could hear the commotion upstairs through the window. I was afraid that we would both learn tonight what it meant to lose a child."

"Did she know what was going on?"

"She was more present than was convenient," Judy said, rolling her eyes in an exaggerated manner in an attempt to make Riley laugh. "But Gabriel had called the cops already. They took us here to get checked out. And we're fine. They just gave me an IV and I felt a lot better."

"I thought they drugged you," Riley replied. "You seemed so out of it."

"They put allergy medicine in some vodka and made me drink it. I didn't know, but it does a number on you."

Allergy medicine in vodka? She used enough allergy meds to know that those things didn't mix. It caused an unbelievable drowsiness, like getting roofied.

It made you black out.

It dawned on Riley that Sierra may had done the same thing to her those nights before she woke up with Brighton.

"I gave birth to a nightmare, didn't I?" Judy asked. Riley frowned.

"I thought you were referring to me for a second. But then I remembered."

"You were a dream," Judy replied. "I was talking about your...*mother.*"

"Sierra – Jujube...whatever her name is," Riley said. "She never was and never will be my mother." She squeezed Judy's hand. "You mothered me enough to last me several lifetimes."

Judy laughed a boisterous laugh. Riley was relieved. Another risky joke.

But it paid off.

44

Gabriel hadn't wanted to leave Riley's side at all, but he had to get home to Penny and Margaret. He figured he'd do that first rather than stick around and spend however much time he'd need to placate Riley and convince her to come with him. Riley didn't seem in a place to be reasoned with.

But then he thought to badger Paul some more.

He called again, offering up cash to find Judy. Paul didn't want to take a job from a man who repeatedly threatened his life, but Gabriel offered to pay double what Judy paid.

And it was then that they realized they weren't talking about the same Judy. And that Paul's Judy was actually Sierra. At which point, Paul informed Gabriel of that phone call that Sierra had forced him to make.

So it turned out Paul wasn't such a bad guy after all.

Together, they concocted a plan. Paul would ask to pick up his final check early since he needed to go out of town. There, he would look to see if anything was out of place. When he saw Riley, he knew there was trouble.

And when he told Gabriel, the wheels turned. He climbed a dumpster and made the leap up to the second floor. He hung from windowsills, swinging his body from each window until he peeked in to find the right one to enter.

To his shock, the third window he looked into contained a small room where Judy sat alone. Tied up.

"And then I got stabbed," Gabriel said, a silly grin on his face. "And then *you* got stabbed!"

He concluded the story from his own hospital bed, clearly still hopped up on some very strong painkillers. Judy had taken Margaret home, leaving Riley alone with Gabriel now. He looked so peaceful for someone who had sustained a pretty bad stab wound.

"Hey, did I hear Sierra say you were pregnant?" Gabriel asked, looking dazed and confused. "Or did I imagine that?" Riley gave him a quick squeeze of his hand.

"She did say that, but I'm not."

"Oh, good," he nodded, considering the fact. Then he turned back towards Riley. "Wanna *get* pregnant?" he teased, a sleepy smile on his face.

"God," Riley smiled. "How charming."

She *was* charmed, though.

EPILOGUE: ONE YEAR LATER

Brighton was what Riley could have been in so many ways.

It upset her to know that he would be punished just as harshly as Sierra. Riley thought that seemed unfair. It was hard for the law to understand what it was like to be under someone's thumb like that. How hard it was to break out of that sort of control.

She was lucky that Evan never coerced her to break the law, although she wondered if it could have come to that. He was a vindictive man and Riley was just another tool in his manipulative arsenal.

There were days where she felt for Sierra too. She was a wayward child who had misconstrued her parents' intentions and carried it with her until it festered into a darkness that couldn't be turned around.

And perhaps there was a genetic element they hadn't considered. Robert had to have suffered quite a mental struggle if he decided his suicide was the best option for everyone. Perhaps Sierra shared that gene with her father – a sensitivity to their difficult surroundings that ultimately wore away at their sanity and souls.

Riley felt for them. She felt for everyone. And she felt it all so hard.

But all that sympathy in Riley's blood wasn't entirely her own doing. It probably had at least *something* to do with the new hormones.

"She can just call me grandma, it's okay!" Judy exclaimed, setting out the milk and sugar for everyone's tea. Riley sat on one side of the dining table with Judy while Gabriel and Margaret sat opposite them.

"But you're not going to be her grandmother, you're going to be her *great* grandmother," Riley said, running her hands over her small baby bump.

"Oh God, that makes me sound so old!" Judy said, scrunching up her nose. "Listen, this is different. This isn't a lie, this is semantics. I will tell her that I am *technically* her great-grandmother, but that it's too much of a mouthful to say all that."

"Fine," Riley rolled her eyes.

"This is all very confusing," Margaret said. "I think we should just stop talking so much and eat, shall we?"

Riley smiled, watching as Gabriel and Margaret dug into their chicken pot pie, completely uninterested in Riley and Judy's silly argument. *Like mother, like son.* Gabriel had no skin in the game on what everyone would be calling everyone. All he knew or cared about was that he'd be called Dad.

And what a great dad he was going to be.

Riley cradled her belly, thinking of the truths her own daughter might need to know one day. Like where Mommy and Daddy's scars come from or the fact that Mommy had been married before. She would have to eventually know about Evan and Sierra and Brighton. She would have to learn about *all* those things one day.

But as Riley watched the peaceful family dinner unfolding before her, she wondered how long she could go without telling her. She wondered if it was even necessary. All she knew was that she would let her daughter live this happy, peaceful future before them for as long as she could possibly let her.

ABOUT THE AUTHOR

Avery Lane is an author of psychological thrillers living in Brooklyn, New York. She spends a lot of time wondering about people's secret lives (and makes up stories for those who insist they don't have one). *Every Step You Take* is her debut novel.

Sign up for Avery's newsletter to get the latest on upcoming titles and ARC opportunities. Don't worry - emails will come sparingly and you can unsubscribe at any time!

Contact
authoraverylane@gmail.com

Made in the USA
Lexington, KY
26 June 2018